A Clue for
CLARA

LIAN TANNER
Illustrated by Cheryl Orsini

ALLEN&UNWIN
SYDNEY·MELBOURNE·AUCKLAND·LONDON

First published by Allen & Unwin in 2020

Allen & Unwin
83 Alexander Street
Crows Nest NSW 2065
Australia
Phone: (61 2) 8425 0100
Email: info@allenandunwin.com
Web: www.allenandunwin.com

A catalogue record for this book is available from the National Library of Australia

ISBN 978 1 76087 769 9

For teaching resources, explore www.allenandunwin.com/resources/for-teachers

Cover and text design by Hannah Janzen
Cover illustration by Cheryl Orsini
Illustrations created in pencil and watercolour on paper
Set in 13/21 pt Archer and Gotham Narrow by Hannah Janzen

Printed in Australia in October 2020 by Griffin Press, part of Ovato

10 9 8 7 6 5 4 3 2

The paper in this book is FSC® certified. FSC® promotes environmentally responsible, socially beneficial and economically viable management of the world's forests.

www.liantanner.com.au

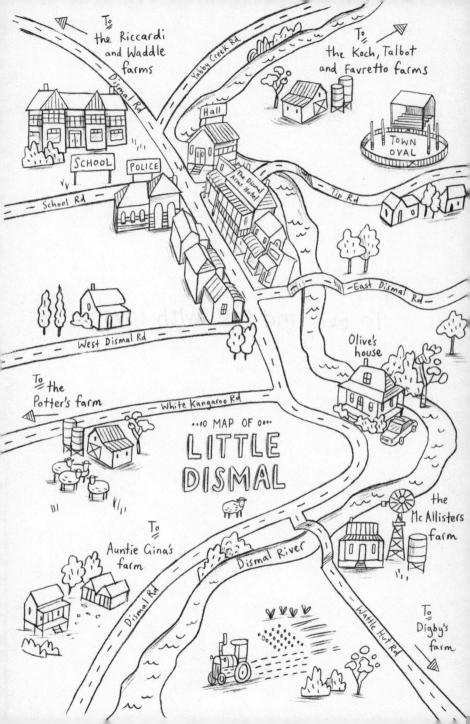

To Evie and Dali, with Love

Monday

5.45 AM

I have groomed my feathers as carefully as I can. I have laid my egg, though it was not yet Egg O'Clock, so the shell was still a bit soft. I have tucked the note under my wing and am standing ready.

My aunts, sisters and cousins are scattered around the yard, scratching for earwigs and chatting to their friends. Rufus is standing on the gatepost, as usual at this time of morning, so he can warn us of hawks, foxes or any other danger. Hopefully, he will crow when he sees the police car.

Today is the day.

7.00 AM

Rufus is handsome and brave, but his eyesight is poor. In the last hour and a quarter he has warned us about a bus, a motorbike and a passing cow.

Through all these false alarms, I hide behind the tractor shed. If my aunts realise what I'm about to do, they will laugh. Then they will pull out another one of my tail feathers. Then they will stop me.

I *will not* be stopped.

8.30 AM

The police car arrives at last, just as the other chooks wander around the corner of the farmhouse and out of sight. Perfect timing. I hurry across the yard, pausing only to snap up a couple of earwigs on the way. (The detectives in the TV show *Death in the City* eat hamburgers. But there are no hamburgers here, so I must improvise.)

The door of the car opens. A police constable steps out, putting on his hat and straightening his belt. I'm about to drop my note next to his big black shoe, when he speaks to someone in the back seat.

'I won't be long,' he says.

'It's okay, Dad,' says the person in the back seat. It sounds like a female voice, though I can't be sure.

But it has given me a name.

Constable Dad strides off towards the farmhouse. I'm about to follow him when

I remember Episode 1 of *Death in the City*, where the uniformed policeman was sent to collect information while the plain-clothes detective, Inspector Garcia, waited in the car. In the *back seat* of the car.

What if that's the case here? What if the person in the back seat is the one in charge? What if I should give my note to her, rather than Constable Dad?

I'm hopping from foot to foot, unable to make up my mind, when Rufus jumps down from the gatepost and struts towards me, puffing out his chest and ruffling his feathers to make himself look bigger. (As well as being handsome, brave and shortsighted, he is also vain. But that's roosters for you.)

'*This is a police car,*' he says in his most important voice, as if I might not have noticed.

I don't think it's right that I'm supposed to make myself small and humble, just because he's a rooster and I'm a chook. But I don't want him getting suspicious, so I lower my head and say, *'Yes, sir.'*

He notices my hopping. *'You've got an egg coming. Off to the nest with you, my girl.'*

(He calls us all 'my girl'. His memory for names is almost as bad as his eyesight.)

'Already done it, sir,' I tell him.

He doesn't believe me. But before he can argue, the back door of the police car opens.

The human in the back seat is very young. Her hair is bound in two long plaits, and her feet are bare.

For a moment, I wonder if I have got it wrong. Then I remember my other favourite TV show, Amelia X, Girl Detective, which I watch with the Boss's

5

favourite grandson, Digby, every Tuesday after school.

Amelia X is a genius, which is how she came to be a detective at such a young age. The girl with plaits in the back seat must be another Amelia X.

Everything rests on this moment, but I daren't do a thing with Rufus watching me. I have to get rid of him.

I lean towards him and murmur, *'Excuse me, sir, but I think I saw a snake go under the house this morning. A big one.'*

Rufus's eyes gleam with excitement. He draws himself up, flaps his wings three times, and runs off, shouting, *'Snake! Snake! Everyone away from the house! Snake! Snake! Snake!'*

He lives for moments like this.

I'm about to fly up onto the car seat and give the girl my note, when the screen door of the farmhouse opens and the Boss comes hurrying over to the car.

'I don't know what Dave was thinking, leaving you out here in the heat,' she says. 'Come inside, Olive dear, come on, I've just made lemonade.'

Another name.

'Hello, Auntie Gina,' says Detective Olive Dear, sliding out of the car and giving the Boss a hug.

Rufus is still shouting. *'Go to the Safe Area, Ladies. I can't protect you if you're wandering around. Snake! Snake! Go to the Safe Area.'*

'What *is* the matter with that rooster?' asks the Boss.

'Don't know,' says the girl. 'He was all right a moment ago.'

I follow them back to the house, and slip past the screen door just before it closes.

The girl says, 'Auntie Gina, there's a chook in the house.'

'That's Clara,' says the Boss. 'She's a scruffy little thing, isn't she? The other chooks bully her, so she dives in here to get away from them. Would you believe she likes to watch television?'

The Boss laughs, which is disappointing. I thought she understood that I was not just *watching television*. I was doing serious research.

Constable Dad is waiting impatiently in the middle of the kitchen, with a letter in his hand. 'So, Gina,' he says. 'You claim you didn't write this?'

'I don't just claim it,' says the Boss, sitting down at the table. 'I *didn't* write it, and I don't know anything about it.'

'There haven't been any egg thefts? None at all?'

'None,' says the Boss.

She's wrong, of course. Last month, a visiting rat stole half a dozen eggs before the Boss could collect them. She didn't know about the rat; she just thought some of the chooks had stopped laying for a couple of days.

But I don't say anything. I've tried for weeks to speak the human language, and I can't get my tongue around it.

Writing is easier. I take the note out from under my wing and drop it next to the girl's bare foot.

'GREETINGS HUMAN,' says the note, in careful black letters. 'I AM LOOKING FOR A MAJOR CRIME TO SOLVE. PLEASE INFORM ME OF ANY RECENT MURDERS, KIDNAPPINGS OR JEWEL HEISTS IN THIS AREA.'

(I would have added something about how I solved the Mystery of the Stolen Eggs, but the scrap of paper wasn't big enough.)

'So this is some sort of prank?' demands Constable Dad, still looking at the letter in his hand. He shakes his head. 'As if I haven't got enough on my plate, with the stock thefts.'

I'm watching the girl closely. Any moment now, she's going to see my note. And because she's a detective (and a genius), she'll realise straight away that the writing on the note is the same as the writing on the letter.

She'll look at me. She'll see the intelligence in my eyes and the ambition in my heart.

And she'll know that the letter isn't a prank. It's a *ploy*. A strategy. It was the only way I could be sure of getting a detective to come to the farm.

I fly up and perch on the back of a chair, so she can see me better.

'Well, come on, Olive,' says Constable Dad. 'I'd better get you to school.'

'It's a public holiday, Dad. Remember?'

'In that case, why don't you stay for another ten minutes?' says the Boss. 'Have a cup of tea.' She fills the jug, talking over her shoulder. 'Did you hear about Ernie Simpson? He's going to sponsor the football team.'

'I heard,' says Constable Dad.

'We would've lost the team, if it wasn't for him,' says the Boss. 'Same with the pub – he bought it just in time. I bless the day he and his daughter arrived in Little Dismal; they were just what we needed.'

Ernie Simpson. I file the name away in my memory, with a question mark against it. Another detective?

The Boss pours hot water into the teapot. 'Actually, I'm glad you came by today, Dave. It's far too long since you dropped in, and you're never home when I visit. You've been working too hard since Maria—'

The girl leaps up, saying, 'I'll get the cups.'

Her bare foot lands on my message and

smears the black letters until they are unreadable.

My beautiful note becomes nothing more than a scrap of dirty paper on the kitchen floor.

Monday

9.00 AM

I have suffered many setbacks in my bid to become a famous detective. My sisters, aunts and cousins have accused me of being a duck in a chook's body. (Everyone knows that ducks are mad.)

The Boss thinks I'm *cute*, which is even more insulting than *duck*. If anyone tried to call Inspector Garcia cute, she would arrest them on the spot.

As for Rufus, he thinks I should spend more time grooming my feathers and improving my eggs.

But I have overcome every setback and I will overcome this one. I *must* overcome it – it is my last hope.

These are the rules of the chookyard:

#1. Get Up Early So You Don't Miss Out.

#2. Keep A Clean House So As Not To Attract Rats.

#3. A Varied Diet Is A Healthy Diet.

But there's a fourth and a fifth rule that no one ever talks about. The fourth rule is this: Beautiful Is Good. Small And Scruffy Is Bad.

I am small and scruffy, which is why I sleep on the bottom perch at night, all by myself. It's why I hide around corners during the day, or dash inside the house to escape from the sharp beaks of my beautiful sisters.

Three months ago, I hoped that the fifth rule might save me. This rule says that if you lay a Beautiful First Egg, everything else will be forgiven. At night, you will be allowed to sit on a higher perch, with warm bodies on either side and no one trying to peck you. In the daytime, you will be part of the flock. You will have friends.

The one I had to impress with my first egg was Grandmother Polly, who rules the yard. (Rufus thinks *he* rules the yard, but everyone knows where the real power lies.) If Grandmother Polly said my first egg was beautiful, everyone else would automatically agree with her.

So there I was, three months ago, standing by the nest, waiting for her verdict.

She was in no hurry to give it.

'You were always an ugly little thing, Clara, right from the moment you hatched,' she squawked, glaring at me out of one bright eye. *'Isabel had a fainting fit when she first saw you, didn't you, Izzy?'*

'You were the horridest chick I'd ever seen,' said Isabel, who is Grandmother Polly's favourite sister. *'I started moulting on the spot,*

which I have never done in all my days. And I've not been completely right since. Oh dear, just the memory of it ...'

She teetered on her long yellow legs, and Grandmother Polly raised a wing and fanned her. *'Steady, Izzy, steady. Think of something nice instead. Think of the egg you laid this morning, one of the best this season. It could very well take out the award for Speckled Beauty.'*

Isabel forgot about fainting, and preened a little. *'It was rather fine, wasn't it? I've been working on the arrangement of the speckles all week, and I've only just got them right.'*

Neither of them had mentioned my egg yet, though it was there on the nest in front of them. It was the first one I'd ever laid, and my whole future rested on it.

I shifted from foot to foot, wondering if I should sing the Egg Song again. But that might make Grandmother Polly think I was too proud, and I wasn't allowed to be even slightly proud until she'd delivered her verdict.

Beautiful or not beautiful?

Just the right size or ridiculously small?

A gorgeous colour or for-heaven's-sake-what-were-you-thinking?

She leaned over the nest and I held my breath. The egg looked beautiful to me. But my opinion wasn't important.

'*Hm,*' said Grandmother Polly. She tilted her head one way, then the other. She tapped the egg gently with her beak. She rolled it over and stared at it again.

Then she looked straight at me and said, '*Too small, very poor shape, completely the wrong colour. Awful. Worst egg I've ever seen.*' And she marched away.

Isabel hurried after her, shouting, '*Clara's egg is awful! Official verdict! Clara's egg is the worst one ever!*'

Everyone else came running from the far

corners of the yard to see what the fuss was about. They stood around the nest, pushing each other to one side so they could see my poor egg.

'It is *awful*,' they said.

'It's *worse than awful. It's embarrassing.*'

'*Are you sure it's even an egg? Maybe she found an ugly old stone, and she's trying to trick us.*'

'*Did she even try to make it beautiful?*'

'*Probably not, you know what she's like.*'

There was a squawk from someone at the back as Rufus pushed his way into the laying shed. '*Make way, make way,*' he cried. '*Rooster coming through. Make way.*'

My sisters, aunts and cousins squeezed to one side, and Rufus stalked up to the nest.

'*Well, my girl,*' he said to me. '*What do you have to say for yourself?*' He didn't wait for an answer, just puffed his chest out a little more and raised his voice to make sure everyone could hear him. *'We're supposed to be a team. We're supposed to pull together, all of us doing our best. But you're letting us down. You're letting us down very badly.'*

There was a murmur of agreement from the other chooks.

I knew what would happen next. Rufus would talk about how useless I was, and how I could do better if I only tried hard enough. Meanwhile, the other chooks would crowd closer and closer. And the minute Rufus stopped speaking, they'd chase me around the farmyard.

So I beat them to it. Before Rufus could say another word, I launched myself into the air and flew out of the laying shed towards the farmhouse.

By the time they came after me, I had dragged the screen door open and hurried inside, where they couldn't follow.

That was a Tuesday morning. Late that

same afternoon, the Boss's grandson Digby and I watched Episode 12 of *Amelia X, Girl Detective*. He had popcorn, which he shared with me. And halfway through the episode, just as Amelia and her trusty dog, Jock, were trying to take back control of a hijacked aeroplane, an idea struck me.

Amelia X was small and scruffy (like me). In the very first episode, the police scoffed at her (just as the other chooks scoff at me), but then she solved a major jewel theft and, with Jock's help, arrested the master criminal behind it.

From that moment on, she was famous. The police were on her side. They respected her. They were her friends.

Inspector Garcia in *Death in the City* had friends, too.

I had nothing except insults and missing tail feathers.

The solution was obvious. Since I would never be beautiful, I must become a famous detective and get my own television show. Then I would have some friends at last.

I immediately started looking for crimes to solve, but it was harder than I expected. Amelia X and Inspector Garcia stumbled across a kidnapping or a murder every time they stepped outside their front door, but I couldn't even find a jewel heist.

When eggs began to disappear from the laying shed, I thought my luck had turned. I solved the crime in a single afternoon, and turned the evidence over to Rufus. Then I waited at the farm gate for the television cameras to arrive.

They did not come. (Which was probably just as well, because by then, Rufus had taken all the credit for himself, and when I tried to tell Grandmother Polly that *I* had solved the mystery, she accused me of lying.)

That's when I realised that I needed a *major* crime. Something important. Something that would make me famous.

Monday

9.30 AM

I have taken three scraps of paper from my secret stash under the verandah. I have scratched through the remains of the old shearing shed, which burnt down a year ago, for another bit of charcoal. Now I'm stationed next to the open door of the police car, preparing to write a new note.

But I've barely set charcoal to paper when a mob of chooks comes storming around the side of the house, their feathers ruffled and their combs wobbling with fury.

'I tell you, there was no snake,' squawks

Grandmother Polly, who is right at the front of the mob, as usual. *'She lied to you, Rufus.'*

'She lied to ME?' says Rufus. *'She tried to make a fool of ME?'*

'She tried to make a fool of all of us. We must teach her a lesson she will not forget.' Grandmother Polly raises her voice. *'Spread out, ladies! We know her usual hiding spots. Raise the alarm if you see her, and cut her off so she can't escape into the house.'*

My heart beats hard and fast inside my chest. This will cost me more than a couple of tail feathers. I have to hide.

But they are already spreading out across the yard, their eyes bright and angry. I can't get to the house, and Grandmother Polly is right, they know all my other hiding spots.

I am lost.

Unless ...

I peep around the car door. There's no sign of Constable Dad or Detective Olive Dear, but the chooks are getting closer and closer.

So I seize the charcoal and the pieces of paper, hop up into the back of the police car and conceal myself behind a large bag on the floor.

9.45 AM

My sisters, aunts and cousins only take notice of the traditional parts of the day. These are:

Pre-dawn, also known as First Squawk.

Proper Dawn, a.k.a. Worm Hunt.

Breakfast O'Clock, a.k.a. Maximum Excitement.

Egg O'Clock, immediately followed by the Egg Song.

Morning Dust Bath.

Scratch O'Clock, a.k.a. Earwig O'Clock.

Nap.

Kitchen Scraps O'Clock, which is almost as important as Breakfast O'Clock.

Afternoon Dust Bath.

General Roaming.

Sundown.

Perch O'Clock, a.k.a. Pushing-and-Shoving, a.k.a. Go-away-Clara-we-don't-like-you.

Last Murmurs.

Dark.

Since my decision to become a detective, however, I have not been satisfied with tradition. With the help of a small wristwatch (which the Boss thinks she lost six weeks ago), and careful observation of the sun, I have become an expert at human time.

So I know that Constable Dad and Detective Olive Dear stay longer than ten minutes.

Unfortunately, they don't stay long enough for Grandmother Polly to call off the search. When the screen door opens, the yard is still filled with angry chooks.

So I do the only thing possible; I stay where I am, inside the police car.

'Are you sure you wouldn't like a casserole to take home?' says the Boss, as Detective Olive Dear and Constable Dad climb into the car.

'No thanks, Gina,' says Constable Dad.

'I do worry about the two of you,' says the Boss. 'I wish you'd let me help.'

'We're fine,' says Constable Dad, starting up the car.

I have a moment of panic, knowing that I'm about to be carried away from the only home I have ever known. And despite everything, it *is* my home, and my sisters, cousins and aunts *are* my sisters, cousins and aunts, even though they treat me badly.

But then it strikes me. This is it. This is my big chance.

Carpe mus!

(Inspector Garcia says *carpe diem*, which means 'seize the day' in Latin. I hate to criticise one of my heroes, but that doesn't make sense. How can you seize a whole day as it dashes past? It doesn't have a tail to grab hold of, or ears. And even if you did manage to grab it, what would you do with it? *Carpe mus* makes a lot more sense. Seize the mouse. And eat it.)

I will seize this chance.

As the police car drives away from the farm, I crouch behind the bag and start work on a different note.

10.00 AM

I know from *Death in the City* that uniformed police officers have to follow orders more closely than plain-clothes detectives do. A uniformed police officer might think it his duty to take me straight back to the farm.

So instead of announcing my presence with a loud squawk, I creep out from behind the bag, and peck the detective's big toe to get her attention.

She stares at me in astonishment, and says, 'Dad, there's a chook—'

I drop my hastily written note onto her lap.

'DON'T GIVE ME AWAY!'

She reads the note, rubs her eyes, then reads it again.

Constable Dad says, over his shoulder, 'What was that?'

'Uh – nothing,' says Detective Olive Dear.

Excellent. I have made contact with a senior plain-clothes detective. Now I must follow up before she loses interest.

The quickest way to communicate is Morse code, which I taught myself from Digby's scout handbook. I begin to tap out a message with my beak, on her bare foot.

'I W-I-S-H T-O—'

I've barely finished the first three words before she jerks her foot away, saying, 'Ow!'

'Are you all right?' asks Constable Dad.

'Um – yes,' says the detective.

I don't think she understands Morse code. So I try semaphore, using my wings as flags.

Right wing goes up at an angle, left wing goes across the body and down. 'I'. Left wing goes up at an angle, right wing goes straight across the body. 'W'.

She's still looking puzzled. So I take a second scrap of paper, pick the charcoal up in my beak and write, **'DON'T YOU UNDERSTAND SEMAPHORE?'**

Her eyes widen. She chews her lip, then shakes her head. In a chook, this would mean, *'The mites are biting me.'* In humans, it means 'No.'

'MORSE CODE?'

Another shake of the head.

This is hard to believe. Amelia X knows semaphore, Morse code, the International Code of Signals, and the ancient African art of the talking drum. In the most recent episode, she was also studying Egyptian hieroglyphics.

I'm beginning to think that Detective Olive Dear might not be a genius after all.

But then she takes something out of the bag. She chews her lip again. She whispers, 'I must be going mad ...'

I look at her closely, to make sure she is not a duck.

She isn't.

I hop up on the seat beside her and inspect the object she's holding. It's a phone.

I know all about phones. They are what humans use to talk to themselves.

If a chook wants to talk to herself, she does it while taking a dust bath. She murmurs quietly; she sings; she remembers the time she caught a mouse under the shearing shed. She doesn't need to hold an object in her claw.

But humans do.

Some of them shout to themselves and wave their arms in the air. Others just hold the phone to their ear, as if they've forgotten what they were going to say.

Even Inspector Garcia talks to herself

sometimes, so I don't hold it against Detective Olive Dear.

But instead of talking to herself, she puts the phone on the seat next to me, and taps it with her finger. Letters appear.

She taps it again, and those letters form words.

'I AM TALKING TO A CHOOK.'

Aha, now I understand. I nudge her hand aside, and peck out my message.

'GREETINGS I AM A DETECTIVE I WISH TO WORK WITH YOU ON AN IMPORTANT CASE A JEWEL HEIST OR A MURDER'

(I can't find the full stop button or the comma, but I think my meaning is clear.)

Detective Olive Dear looks at what I have written. Her eyes widen even further. She puts her hand over her mouth and makes a choking sound.

I peck at the letters again.

'HAVE YOU BEEN EATING PLUM PIPS
OR LARGE SCRAPS OF BREAD THEY ARE
VERY BAD FOR CHOKING'

(I can't find the question mark either.)

She shakes her head. 'No.' Then she closes her eyes and whispers, 'I'm definitely going mad.'

'YOU ARE NOT A DUCK,' I write, just in case she was worried.

'Um,' says the detective.

But before she can reply to my message, Constable Dad stops the car. I dive into the bag, wriggle under a couple of books and keep very still (just like Amelia X in Episode 3, when she and Jock hid in a wardrobe to escape from an international gang of kidnappers).

Detective Olive Dear picks up the bag with me in it, climbs out of the car, and carries the bag into a house.

10.15 AM

'Chook?' says Detective Olive Dear. 'You can come out now.'

I wriggle out from under the books and look around carefully. There is a stove, just like the one at the farm. There is a refrigerator. There is a table with four chairs.

There is also a sink full of dirty dishes, an overflowing rubbish bin, and a feeling of sadness about the place. (A bit like the sadness of a broken egg, when you've gone to so much trouble to lay it.)

I fly up onto the back of one of the chairs, and the detective sits on the end of the table, with her phone beside her.

'So … chook,' she says.

I hop over to the phone, and tap out 'CLARA'. 'You're the one who likes to watch TV, right? Yes, of course you are. So, Clara, what's this about?'

'YOU ARE A GENIUS YES?' (I have

found the question mark. The comma is still missing.)

Detective Olive Dear pulls a face. 'What? No!'

I look up at her. 'YOURE NOT A GENIUS?'

She laughs unhappily. 'No.'

This calls for a rethink. I scratch behind my ear, then I write, 'WHAT CASE ARE YOU WORKING ON?'

She reads the message, and blinks. 'Case? What do you mean?'

She's right when she says she is not a genius. Amelia X would have snapped out the answer without hesitation. But I do not give up.

'HOW OLD ARE YOU?'

'Eleven. Last week.'

That would be old for a chicken. But not for a human.

'HOW DID YOU BECOME A DETECTIVE AT SUCH A YOUNG AGE IF YOU ARE NOT A GENIUS?'

'A detective?' she says. 'I'm not a detective.

I don't know where you got all these weird ideas from.'

For a moment, I am overwhelmed with dismay (just like Inspector Garcia in Episode 9, when she discovered that the new police recruit was the son of her old enemy, Half-Tongue Harry).

But like Inspector Garcia, I do not give up. I straighten my pin feathers, bob my head, and bend over the phone.

'TAKE ME TO CONSTABLE DAD.' (I have found the full stop.)

'You want to see Dad? Why – oh, right. The detective thing. Um, Clara, I'm not sure that Dad can help you.'

'WHY NOT?'

'He's really busy at the moment, with the stock thefts and – and stuff.'

'I WISH TO WORK WITH HIM. I HAVE TRAINED MYSELF IN ALL ASPECTS OF DETECTING.'

The phone is better than paper, because it doesn't run out of room. 'I HAVE STUDIED THE SCIENCE OF CLAW PRINTS. I CAN TRACE A FEATHER BACK TO ITS OWNER EVEN IF IT HAS BEEN SITTING OUT IN THE RAIN FOR A WEEK. I KNOW MORSE CODE AND SEMAPHORE AND AM LEARNING EGYPTIAN HIEROGLYPHICS.'

That last bit is not entirely true, because Digby's scout handbook doesn't have a section on hieroglyphics.

But as soon as I find a book that *does* have them, I will learn them.

When ~~Detective~~ Olive Dear has read everything I've written, I add the most important bit. 'IT WAS I WHO SOLVED THE MYSTERY OF THE STOLEN EGGS.'

Then I stand back, knowing how impressed she must be. (I don't tell her that Rufus killed the rat thief. I don't know how she feels about capital punishment.)

She pulls out a chair and sits down. 'Look, Clara. I'm sure you're really clever—'

I nod my head in agreement.

'But it's no use taking you to the police station. Dad won't let you help. He won't let *any*one help.'

She looks so sad that I wonder if she has broken an egg recently. I am sad too, and disappointed. My plan is not working.

But Every Challenge Is Also An Opportunity (Inspector Garcia, Episode 4). I flutter over to the sink and start picking scraps of beans and toast off the dirty dishes. (I always think better when I'm eating. And besides, it's been a long time since Breakfast O'Clock.)

When I have eaten my fill, I fly back to the table, where the phone is waiting.

'So do you want to go back to the farm?' asks ~~Det~~ Olive Dear.

'NO!!!!!!!!!' (I have found the exclamation mark.)

'I could take you there on my bike, if you like.'

'I AM NOT GOING TO THE FARM,' I write. 'PLEASE OPEN THE BACK DOOR.'

12.30 PM

While Olive does human things, I make a detailed investigation of the compost heap. Then I scratch up a bit of lawn just in time for Afternoon Dust Bath.

I settle down with my wings spread and my eyes half closed, and scoop dust into my feathers, all around the itchy bits. And I do some more thinking. In particular, I think about Amelia X and Jock, her faithful sidekick.

By the time Olive comes out to the garden to find me, I know what to do.

'IF THE POLICE DO NOT WANT MY HELP,' I write, 'WE WILL HAVE TO GO FREELANCE.'

'We?' says Olive.

'I AM A DETECTIVE,' I write.

'Oka-ay.'

'SO I WILL BE IN CHARGE AND YOU WILL BE MY FAITHFUL SIDEKICK.'

Olive chews her thumbnail. 'Thanks for the offer, Clara, but I'm – um – a bit busy right now. You go ahead with the detective stuff if you want.'

Another disappointment.

I scoop up some more dust. Perhaps I don't need a faithful sidekick. After all, Inspector Garcia doesn't have one, and her record of arrests is even better than Amelia's. (Inspector Garcia *does* have a trusty driver, Sergeant Bell, but I will do without a driver for now.)

'Are you sure you don't want to go back to the farm?' says Olive.

'I AM SURE.'

'So you're staying here?'

'I AM STAYING.'

I wait for her cries of joy. They do not come.

Tuesday

5.30 AM

I slept in the wardrobe, and dreamt of mad scientists and a secret formula hidden inside a stuffed teddy bear (*Amelia X*, Episode 2). Now it is Pre-dawn, or First Squawk. Time for the day to begin.

Olive is still asleep, so I flap down off the wardrobe rail, and onto the bed. If my sisters, aunts and cousins were here, we would all do First Squawk together. It is the one time of day when I am truly part of the flock.

I feel a moment of sadness – but it is quickly replaced by excitement. The great adventure has begun, and no one has pecked me since yesterday.

As a special treat, I will let Olive join me in greeting the morning. I hop up onto the pillow and do First Squawk in her ear.

She is no longer asleep.

'What did you do that for?' cries Olive, sitting up in bed.

I look around for the phone, so I can answer her, but I can't find it.

She fumbles for the clock on her bedside table. 'It's half past five! What are you doing waking me up at half past five? Go away.'

She lies down again and closes her eyes.

'*Get up get up,*' I squawk, and I quote the first rule of the chookyard. '*Get Up Early So You Don't Miss Out.*'

She throws her pillow at me. I dodge. She throws the clock at me. I dodge again (just as Inspector Garcia dodged a hail of bullets in Episode 11 of *Death in the City*).

I'm beginning to think that Olive is not a morning person.

But at last she takes her phone out from under the bedclothes and pushes it towards me.

'I NEED A LIST OF RECENT UNSOLVED CRIMES,' I write.

Olive cracks her eyes open and reads my message. 'You mean here in Little Dismal?' she mumbles. 'Um – there's not a lot of crime. Only the stock thefts. And Dad's working on those.' She yawns. 'I'm going back to sleep. Goodnight.'

I nudge her with the claw. 'OTHER CRIMES?'

Before she can answer, her phone buzzes. Olive looks at it and her face goes red. She throws the phone across the room and burrows under the bedclothes.

As her head disappears, I hear her mumble, 'I'll tell you what's a crime. That people still think Jubilee Crystal Simpson is a decent human being. That's a crime. That's a *real* crime.'

And just like that, I learn the name of Little Dismal's master criminal.

6.15 AM

Egg O'Clock. I wander around the garden looking for a safe, comfortable spot, before settling under a bush. There's no straw, but I find some grass and leaves, which I pull together into a nest. Then I sit down and pore over the problem of Jubilee Crystal Simpson.

Dealing with a master criminal is no easy matter. First, I must find her secret hide-out (*Amelia X*, Episode 3), and set up an observation post to watch her and her gang. I must install hidden cameras. I must follow the gang members wherever they go. And only then, when I know where all the bodies are buried, will I be able to arrest them.

By the time I've worked it out, the egg has come. It is not very big, or very beautiful, but it is mine, and because the Boss is not here to collect it, it will still be here tomorrow. I sing the Egg Song, and head for a different part of the yard for Morning Dust Bath and Scratch

O'Clock. I must get them all out of the way early today, so I can start my investigations.

8.00 AM

I'm sitting on the windowsill, planning my first move, when Constable Dad stumbles into the kitchen wearing his uniform.

Like Olive, he is not a morning person. He makes coffee, toast and beans, which, judging from the dishes in the sink, is the same as he and Olive ate last night.

(They have obviously never learned the third rule of the chookyard, A Varied Diet Is A Healthy Diet.)

Constable Dad eats his breakfast. Then he leans back in his chair, and water comes out of his eyes.

When the tap in the Boss's garden leaks like that, the Boss gets a large spanner and hits the tap several times. If that doesn't work, she tightens it until it stops leaking.

I look around the kitchen for a spanner, but can't find one. So I fly over to the table and catch the water in my beak as it drips off his face. I'm thirsty, and there is no point wasting it.

Constable Dad stares down at me. 'A chook? Now I'm imagining things. Or maybe I'm going mad.'

'You are NOT a duck,' I tell him. (Why do I have to keep saying this? Haven't these people ever *seen* a duck? Don't they know that ducks don't wear clothes or drink coffee?)

Constable Dad pats me gingerly. 'At least you're a nice hallucination. Maria would've – she would've liked you.'

He leaks a bit more, but before I can catch it, he brushes the water away from his eyes, pushes his plate towards me, and stands up. 'Pull yourself together, Dave,' he mutters. 'You've got work to do.'

I know he's not talking to me, because my name is not Dave. So he must be talking to himself. But why is he calling himself Dave when his name is Dad? I wish I had a phone, so I could ask him.

I could ask him about master criminal Jubilee Crystal Simpson at the same time. Where is her hide-out? How many people are in her gang? Does she have a mole in the police department?

(I was confused when Inspector Garcia first mentioned moles in Episode 13 of *Death in the City*. The Boss's dictionary describes them as 'small animals that live underground. They have velvety fur, very small ears and eyes, and short, powerful front legs for digging.'

'Why would a criminal send a mole into the police department?' I asked the television. But then I realised. To dig up evidence with its powerful front legs. And destroy it.)

8.20 AM

Olive appears in the kitchen and mumbles at Constable Dad. Then he goes to work. Olive stands at the kitchen window and watches him drive away, and *her* eyes begin to leak too.

Still no spanner.

8.35 AM

Olive is packing books into her bag. 'You can hang around the house today if you want,' she says. 'I'll leave the window open.'

'Where are you going?' I squawk.

She gets her phone out of the bag and puts it on the table. 'There. What did you say?'

'WHERE ARE YOU GOING?'

'To school.'

'WHILE YOU ARE GONE I WILL FIGHT CRIME.'

Olive pulls a face. 'Lucky you. Fighting crime has to be better than going to school with Jubilee Crystal Simpson.'

The master criminal is at *school*?

I almost knock the phone off the table in my excitement. 'I HAVE CHANGED MY MIND. I WILL GO WITH YOU.'

'You can't. No, don't argue, there's no way I can take you with me.' She turns away, muttering, 'Where are my shoes?'

In Episode 15 of *Amelia X*, a criminal gang took over an Antarctic base and held the scientists hostage. The high-ranking Interpol officer sent to bring the gang to justice refused to have Amelia and Jock on his team, even though one of the scientists was Amelia's uncle. So she and her sidekick stowed away on the icebreaker, with a two-week supply of emergency rations and dog biscuits.

While Olive is out of the room looking for her shoes, I grab a slice of toast from the table and dive into her schoolbag. By the time she returns, the toast and I are hidden under her books.

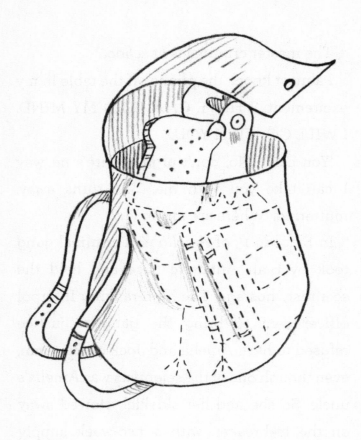

'Clara?' she calls.

I squat at the bottom of the bag and say nothing.

'Clara?' she calls again. 'I'll see you after school.' Then she picks up the bag and carries me outside.

8.50 AM

School is like a yard full of chooks, with all of them squawking and cackling at the same time. The only one not making any noise is Olive.

She walks past the noisy children, and they fall silent. All except one. A familiar voice calls out, 'Hey, Olive.'

I almost leap out of the bag with excitement. It's the Boss's grandson, Digby! Here, at school!

Olive mumbles, 'Hey, Digby,' and keeps walking.

A bell rings. The squawking starts up again, only now it's moving along with Olive, pushing past her and jostling her bag.

We enter a building. Olive sets the bag down and I freeze, as if there is a hawk flying overhead.

Other human children drop their bags near mine and I discover, through listening to their cackles, that we are in something called a locker room. After they drop their bags, they head for the classroom next door.

Olive takes out a couple of books and a pencil case, and leaves.

I stay where I am, not moving.

Well, not moving *very much*. My emergency rations are squashed up against my beak, so I nibble them while I wait for something to happen.

Amelia X and Jock stayed where they were while three members of the criminal gang sneaked onto the icebreaker in the middle of the night to capture its crew.

'We're still gathering information about these villains, Jock,' whispered Amelia. 'The time is not yet ripe to act.'

I eat a little more of my emergency rations, and wonder if Jubilee Crystal Simpson will send members of *her* gang to capture Olive's schoolbag.

At last my patience pays off. Two children enter the locker room. At first, they are the same as all the others, talking loudly about unimportant things.

But then their voices sink to a whisper. I hear a rustling sound, like a rat stealing eggs from a nest. Someone giggles. Someone whispers, 'Over here, Jubilee.' And a hand drops something into Olive's bag, right above my head.

Jubilee! The master criminal is here!

I am as still as an iceberg.

No, *more* still, because icebergs float.

I am as still as a non-floating iceberg.

Another giggle, somewhere above me. Then two sets of footsteps walk away. A door closes. Silence falls on the locker room.

I pick up what's left of my emergency rations, nudge the books to one side, and poke my head through the gap. Something is tucked down the side of the books. Something that wasn't there earlier.

I wriggle out of the bag and look around for a hiding place. There's a cupboard in the corner with a pile of boxes next to it, so I tuck my rations behind the boxes, then hurry back to inspect the *something*.

It is a small pink purse.

Chooks do not use purses. If we did, we'd keep sensible things in them, like dead mice, or strawberries. We certainly wouldn't bother with bits of paper and shiny stones.

However, I know that humans value those bits of paper and shiny stones. And when I realise that Jubilee Crystal Simpson has put them in Olive's bag, I smell a rat.

(Not an *actual* rat. If I smelled an *actual* rat, I'd be up on top of the cupboard already, squawking for help. Mice are small and edible. Rats are big and creepy, and Rufus is the only one who can kill them.)

But like Amelia X, I am still gathering information. The time is not yet ripe to act.

So I leave the purse in Olive's schoolbag, creep behind the boxes, and set to work finishing off my emergency rations.

10.15 AM
It's a long, slow morning, and I miss Morning Dust Bath. I do Nap instead, and dream of Grandmother Polly and how she will like me when I am famous, and invite me to sleep on the top perch with her.

She's just telling me how wonderful I am, and apologising for all the times she pecked me, when I am woken by the thunder of footsteps.

The door flies open and the human children burst into the locker room. They're bustling around, chattering, when a shriek cuts through all the noise.

'My purse! Where's my purse? Mrs Savage, someone's stolen my purse!'

More footsteps, heavier than the children's. 'Just because you can't find something,

Tracy, doesn't mean someone stole it. Now, which is your bag?'

'That one. And someone *must* have stolen it, Mrs Savage, because it was there this morning. I saw it just before I came into class.'

'What colour is it?' asks Mrs Savage.

'Pink,' says Tracy. 'I was almost the last person in the locker room. The only one who came after me was Olive Hennessey.'

'I didn't come after you,' Olive says quietly.

'Yes, you did,' says Tracy. 'I know we have to be nice to you, Olive, because of your mum. But that doesn't mean we should cover it up when you do something wrong. And you *did* steal Pippa's new pen last week, and you should have got into trouble for that—'

She's interrupted by a new voice. It is not like the other voices. I believe it is called a Merrycan accent. 'I hope you're not suggesting that poor Olive took your purse.'

'Of course she's not, Jubilee,' says Mrs Savage.

'Because poor Olive wouldn't do that sort of thing,' says Jubilee. 'I *know* she wouldn't, and I'm sure the thing with Pippa's new pen was just a mistake, and if you're going to make up lies about her, Tracy, then I won't be your friend anymore.'

'I'm *not* making up lies,' cries Tracy. 'I just—'

Mrs Savage raises her voice. 'Let's not be melodramatic, girls. No one is suggesting—'

'I'll prove it wasn't Olive. You don't mind if I look in your bag, do you, Olive?' Jubilee doesn't wait for an answer. I hear the thump of books being turfed out onto the floor.

Silence.

Then, 'Oh,' says Jubilee. 'Oh, Olive. It *was* you.' She sounds disappointed and puzzled.

'I told you so,' says Tracy.

'I didn't take it,' mumbles Olive.

'Of course you did,' says Tracy. 'You're a thief, Olive Hennessey, and—'

'Now, Tracy,' says Jubilee, 'that's just not fair. I'm sure Olive didn't mean to steal your purse – she just had a sort of fit or something. Because of—'

'That's enough,' says Mrs Savage. 'Olive, I'll talk to you after school. Tracy, you shouldn't have left your purse in the locker room in the first place. I've told you about this before.'

'I thought it was safe,' says Tracy. 'I didn't realise there was a thief in our—'

Mrs Savage interrupts her. 'I said that's *enough*! Now get what you need and go back to the classroom.'

There's a general shuffling of feet. A voice says, 'It might not have been Olive who took your purse, Tracy.' It's Digby, the Boss's grandson. 'Anyone might have moved it. You might have done it yourself.'

'Don't be dumb, I'm hardly going to steal my own purse,' snaps Tracy. 'You're just saying that because she's your cousin, Digby—'

Anyone still in this locker room in twenty seconds will stay behind after school and clean the toilets. One ... Two ... Three ...'

When the stampede has died away and the locker room is quiet again, I peck at the last few crumbs of emergency rations and think about the information I have gathered.

1. Tracy is part of Jubilee Crystal Simpson's gang.

2. Digby is not. (Which is a relief. If I arrested him, he would not give me any more popcorn.)

3. Mrs Savage is not. (Which is also a relief. She is almost as fierce as Grandmother Polly.)

4. As for Jubilee Crystal Simpson herself, she is indeed a master criminal, and a very clever one.

As soon as I find out where her secret hide-out is, I will start searching for the bodies she has buried and the jewels she has stolen.

Then the TV cameras will come, and I will be famous.

3.30 PM

Olive searches her bag to make sure there's nothing in it that shouldn't be there, and finds me hiding under her books, ready to go home.

'Oh Clara,' she says, shaking her head. She has been talking to Mrs Savage and her eyes are red.

She picks up her bag with me in it and goes to fetch her bike.

The ride home is not a comfortable one.

4.30 PM

'Jubilee pretends she's on my side,' says Olive. 'She says, "Oh no, Olive wouldn't steal, I know she wouldn't." But then somehow she always ends up searching my schoolbag, or my desk, and finding something that someone's lost.

And then she pretends to be really sympathetic and sad about it, when she's probably the one who put it there in the first place.'

'SHE DID,' I write on the phone.

'You saw her?' Olive has been lying on her bed, but now she sits up. 'I knew it! I knew it was her.'

'AND TRACY.'

'I hate them so much. I wish I could prove it was them.'

'IN EPISODE 12 OF DEATH IN THE CITY,' I write, 'HALF-TONGUE HARRY PUT A HEROINE IN INSPECTOR GARCIA'S CAR TO GET THE INSPECTOR INTO TROUBLE.'

'Put a what?'

'A HEROINE. A BRAVE FEMALE. IN A SMALL PLASTIC BAG.'

Olive almost smiles for the first time since we came home. 'Not *a* heroine. Just *heroin*. It's an illegal drug.'

'IT'S NOT A PERSON?'

'No.'

That explains a lot. I thought at the time that she must have been a very *small* brave female. Or that perhaps she had run out onto the road, like my cousin Floss, and gotten squashed.

Wednesday

5.30 AM

My second day as a proper detective. I fly down from my perch in the wardrobe and land on the end of the bed. Olive is still asleep. Her phone is nowhere to be seen.

   She was unhappy last night, so I decide to let her sleep in this morning.

5.35 AM

That should be enough extra sleep. I hop up onto the pillow and let her share First Squawk.

   'Aaaaargh!' she screams, and falls out of bed.

   The extra sleep has not made her any happier.

'Go *away*, Clara,' she says. 'Leave me alone!'

She snatches up the phone so I can't answer her, climbs back into bed, and pulls the covers over her head. I hurry outside for Proper Dawn.

6.20 AM

Egg O'Clock. I settle under the same bush as yesterday and spend a pleasant half-hour daydreaming about the time when I will have my own television show.

Then I have an early Scratch O'Clock, followed by a quick Dust Bath.

Today I will go to school and watch Jubilee Crystal Simpson more closely. And when she leaves school I will follow her to her secret hide-out.

8.20 AM

Constable Dad has gone to work and Olive is in the kitchen eating beans and toast. To my dismay, she says, 'You can't come to school with me today, Clara. You should be outside doing – um – chook things. I'll see you this afternoon.'

I argue, but she will not change her mind.

8.35 AM

How did she know I was hiding in her schoolbag again? She is smarter than I thought.

8.38 AM

How did she know I had sneaked up onto the back of her bicycle? She is *much* smarter than I thought.

8.40 AM

I try to follow Olive's bike, so I can collect more information on Jubilee Crystal Simpson. But she goes too fast and leaves me behind.

If Amelia X was here, she would hail a taxi and cry, 'Follow that bicycle!' But although I wait and wait, not a single taxi goes past.

I decide that it is time to have a proper talk with Constable Dad. Perhaps he already knows the location of the master criminal's secret hide-out.

10.00 AM

Little Dismal does not have traffic lights. And although I have walked the length of the main street, I have not seen a single shootout. Or a drug raid. Apart from that, it is just like the city where Inspector Garcia lives. It has cars. It has shops. It has humans. But none of them appear to be dangerous criminals, which is disappointing.

I find the police station easily enough, near the end of the main street. Constable Dad's hat is on his desk, but Constable Dad is nowhere to be seen.

I flutter up onto his desk, looking for information about Jubilee Crystal Simpson. But all I can find is reports on stock thefts.

I know all about stock. It is a type of soup. The Boss makes chicken stock (which is soup for chickens) and beef stock (which is soup for beefs). I have no idea why Constable Dad is so worried about someone stealing soup. When he comes back, I will suggest he work on more important matters.

To amuse myself while I wait, I decide to try on his police hat. I lift the edge of it with my beak, and crawl underneath. The hat falls around me.

And suddenly it is nighttime!

I have never known darkness to come so early in the day. Usually it waits until the end of the afternoon.

I have also never known it to come so

quickly. Usually it is a slow thing, with time to snap up one last earwig, then wander back to the coop behind my sisters. Usually there are Last Murmurs and Pushing-and-Shoving and You're-not-allowed-on-this-perch-Clara, and Rufus and Grandmother Polly still bossing us around as the sun goes down.

But things are clearly different in Little Dismal.

I should have expected it.

I do my own Last Murmurs, and settle down to sleep. But I've barely closed my eyes when I hear footsteps. They do not sound like Constable Dad's footsteps, but who else would visit a police station at night?

The mysterious visitor walks around to the other side of the desk and shuffles through the information on stock thefts. (Apparently Constable Dad is not the only one interested in soup.) Then they leave.

I close my eyes and go to sleep.

NEXT MORNING
(I THINK)

Someone picks up the hat – and it is morning already! Even though I have only slept for a few minutes.

What a strange place this is.

I do First Squawk all on my own. (It is not nearly as enjoyable as usual. For the first time since I left the farm, I miss my sisters, even the nastiest ones.)

A voice above me says, '*Another* chook? Or are you the same one? Well, it's a fairly harmless hallucination, I suppose.'

And Constable Dad sits down and starts to shuffle through the reports.

I look around for his phone, so I can ask him about Jubilee Crystal Simpson's hide-out. But I can't find it. I try Morse code instead, tapping out my message on the desk.

'Are you hungry, chook?' he asks, without

looking up from his papers. 'Go out the back, I'm sure there are worms in the garden.'

(I am reminded of Episode 10 of *Amelia X*, in which she and Jock travelled to a remote part of China. Amelia speaks Chinese, of course, but these people spoke a different sort of Chinese, and she couldn't make herself understood until she found someone who knew the International Code of Signals.)

I search for a bit of charcoal, but all I can find is a pen. It is harder to use than charcoal, but I pick it up in my beak and prepare to write my message on the corner of Constable Dad's report.

The pen slips, and a black mark zips right across the middle of the paper.

Constable Dad looks up, frowning. 'Hallucination or not, you have to go,' he says. And without even asking my permission, he picks me up, carries me through the police station, and tosses me out into the garden.

I try to rush back inside, but he shuts the door in my face.

'Is this any way to treat a detective?' I squawk.

He doesn't answer.

I'm just wondering if I should do Proper Dawn (a.k.a. Worm Hunt) while I'm out here, when I notice the position of the sun.

It is completely wrong. The shadows are wrong, too. It is not Proper Dawn at all. It is – I check the sun again and make some quick calculations. It is ...

It is 12.30 PM already!

I have no idea where the earlier parts of the day went. Perhaps time works differently in Little Dismal. Perhaps the nights are only a few minutes long, and dawn is missed out entirely.

I hurry around to the front of the police station and go in through the door. Constable Dad is talking to himself on the phone.

No, wait. I used a phone to talk to Olive. So maybe that's what Constable Dad is doing. Talking to *someone else*!

'Yes, sir,' he says. 'No, sir, not yet ... I'm pretty sure they're the same people who were stealing stock in northern New South Wales last year ... No, I can't prove it, sir.'

I peer around the office, but there's no sign of Sir. Could he be *inside the phone*?

Constable Dad pulls a face. 'Yes, sir, it *is* taking me longer than expected to make an arrest. If you could just sign off on those CCTV cameras, sir ... Yes, sir, I understand there's no money, but ... Yes, sir, I know other stations are doing it tough ... Hard for all of us, yes, sir, but if I could just have a *few* cameras, sir ...'

He sits bolt upright. '*What?* I mean, no, sir, there's absolutely no need to replace me, I'm doing everything that can be done ... No, I'm sure another person wouldn't get a result any quicker, sir ... Pressure from above, yes, sir, I understand you're in a difficult position, but no one else knows this area like I do, sir ... No, sir, I don't need a holiday ... Yes, sir, I'll do without the cameras ... Yes, I'm sure I'll make an arrest soon, sir ... I hope so, too. Thank you, sir.'

He puts the phone down. Then he leans forward, rests his head on the desk and groans.

12.40 PM

This is disturbing news. If Constable Dad is replaced, he will leave town, and Olive will leave with him.

I will have nowhere to live. I might even have to go back to the farm.

The mere thought of it makes my feathers twitch. I decide to spend the rest of the day searching the town for the missing soup.

3.30 PM

I don't find it.

4.30 PM

Olive is lying on her bed, staring at the ceiling. I hop up beside her and peck out a message on her phone.

'CONSTABLE DAD IS IN TROUBLE,' I write.

Olive reads the message and sits up. 'What do you mean?'

'SIR WANTS TO REPLACE HIM BECAUSE HE CAN'T SOLVE THE STOCK THEFTS.'

'What? How do you know?'

'I HEARD HIM TALKING TO HIS PHONE AT THE POLICE STATION. CAN HE SOLVE THE STOCK THEFTS?'

'Of course he can,' says Olive. 'It takes a while, that's all, because the farms are so spread out. And the thieves are really clever. But Dad'll get there, especially once they give him the cameras he asked for.'

'THEY WON'T GIVE HIM THE CAMERAS.'

'They won't?' says Olive. 'Well then, he'll still get there. It might just take a bit longer.'

But she looks worried.

'WOULD SOMEONE ELSE GET THERE QUICKER?'

'No! At least, I don't think so.' She chews her thumbnail. 'This is awful, Clara. He's working so hard on the stock thefts. How can they even think of replacing him?'

That's when I decide to ask her the question that has been bothering me all day. 'WHY IS EVERYONE SO WORRIED ABOUT SOUP?'

'Soup?' says Olive, looking puzzled.

'SOUP,' I write again.

'Why are we talking about soup?' she asks.

My cousin Gladys used to do this. She'd be in the middle of a conversation about earwigs, and she'd suddenly stop and say, *Why are we talking about earwigs? Why don't we discuss something important, like the meaning of life?*

She called herself a philosopher. *I* think it was because she was dropped on her head soon after she came out of the egg.

'WERE YOU DROPPED ON YOUR HEAD?'
I write.

'What?'

'NEVER MIND. WHY ARE THEY WORRIED ABOUT SOUP?'

'They're not. They're worried about the stock thefts—' She breaks off. She puts her hand over her mouth.

'Clara,' she says carefully. 'Stock *can* mean soup. But it also means farm animals. Like sheep.'

Now I'm the one who is puzzled. Sheep are useless animals. They don't even lay eggs. 'WHO WOULD STEAL SHEEP?' I ask.

'These are valuable sheep,' says Olive. 'They've been going missing for weeks, and no one knows who's taking them.'

I have a tingling feeling in my chest. It might be fleas. But it might also be excitement. Disappearing sheep? Disappearing *valuable* sheep? And no one knows who's taking them?

At last! Here is a crime worthy of my talents!

What's more, I've already solved it.

'TAKE ME TO CONSTABLE DAD,' I write.

'Why?'

'I WISH TO TELL HIM WHO IS STEALING THE VALUABLE SHEEP.'

Olive stares at me. 'But you can't possibly know. A moment ago, you thought they were soup.'

I sigh. 'SOMEONE IS STEALING SHEEP?'

Olive nods.

'AND THAT SOMEONE IS A CRIMINAL?'

Another nod.

'A MASTER CRIMINAL?'

'Maybe. Maybe not.'

Of course it is a master criminal. It is *always* a master criminal. (This is why I am the detective, and Olive is not. I know these things. She doesn't.)

'WHO IS THE MASTER CRIMINAL IN LITTLE DISMAL?'

I was hoping she would have worked it out

for herself by now. But she hasn't. So I tell her.

'JUBILEE CRYSTAL SIMPSON.'

Olive stares at me with her mouth hanging open. (If she was a chook, this would mean she was sick. I'm not sure what it means for humans.)

'You think Jubilee Crystal ...' She shakes her head. 'I wish she *was* a master criminal, so she'd go to jail and leave me alone. But she's not. She's just a nasty person. Except I'm the only one who thinks she's nasty, because she's really pretty and she's good at sport and her father bought the Little Dismal pub three months ago to save it from closing. And now Mr Simpson is going to sponsor the footy team. So everyone thinks she's wonderful.'

'YOU DO NOT BELIEVE JUBILEE CRYSTAL SIMPSON IS STEALING THE VALUABLE SHEEP?'

'She's just a kid,' says Olive. 'You need trucks and stuff to steal sheep. It's adults, not kids.'

6.00 PM

Beans on toast again. (Don't these people know anything about a healthy diet? Where are the snails? Where are the little crunchy spiders? Where are the earwigs?)

Olive looks at her plate and sighs. 'Dad,' she says.

Constable Dad has another pile of papers beside his plate, and is scribbling on the top one. 'Mm?' he says, without looking up.

'Maybe I could cook tomorrow night,' says Olive, poking the beans with her fork.

'I don't mind cooking,' says Constable Dad. He crosses something out and writes over the top of it. 'You've got your homework and your friends. I know you're busy.'

'But I could make something different ...' Her voice trails off.

Constable Dad looks up and sees me sitting on the back of Olive's chair. He blinks. 'Why am I suddenly seeing chooks all over the place?'

'Um – this is Clara,' says Olive.

'Where did she come from?' asks Constable Dad.

'Auntie Gina's farm.'

'Does Gina know she's here?'

'Probably not.'

'Then you'd better phone her.'

'Okay. But Dad, about cooking—'

'You don't like beans?'

'I love them,' Olive says quickly. 'It's just—'

'That's all right then,' says Constable Dad. 'Don't forget to phone Gina.' And he goes back to his work.

9.00 PM

Olive's eyes are leaking, and she is making strange noises. Even though it is well past Perch O'Clock, I fly out of the wardrobe onto her bed to see if she needs a spanner.

When I land on the pillow beside her, she whispers, 'What am I going to do, Clara?

All Dad thinks about is work, and now that's going wrong too. I don't *want* him to be sent somewhere else. I've lived in Little Dismal all my life, and – and Mum's family are here, Auntie Gina and Auntie Mel and Uncle Tony and the rest of them. And even with Jubilee being so horrible and turning people against me, I couldn't bear to leave. What am I going to *do*?'

The answer is obvious. I'm surprised she hasn't seen it already. 'WE MUST HELP CONSTABLE DAD SOLVE THE SOUP—' *delete soup* '—STOCK THEFTS. THEN HE WILL NOT HAVE TO GO AND NEITHER WILL YOU.'

'But how can we help him? I'm just a kid. And you're a chook. I mean, you're a *nice* chook. But ...'

I answer her doubts with a direct quote from Amelia X. 'WE CAN GO PLACES THE POLICE CANNOT GO. WE CAN SEE THINGS THEY DO NOT SEE. THE

CRIMINALS WILL NEVER SUSPECT THAT WE ARE AFTER THEM.'

Olive sniffs a couple of times. 'Are you serious?'

'I AM SERIOUS.'

She takes a piece of cloth from under her pillow and blows her nose. 'Maybe you're right. I'm sure Dad doesn't really need help – but maybe three heads are better than one.'

'SO WE WILL INVESTIGATE?'

'I guess so.'

'AND YOU WILL BE MY FAITHFUL SIDEKICK?'

'Um – okay.'

I feel like running around the room, flapping my wings and squawking with excitement. But Olive interrupts me.

'Do you think I should tell Dad we're working on this?' she asks.

'NO,' I write. 'WE DO NOT GIVE OUT INFORMATION UNLESS SOMEONE

GIVES US SOMETHING IN RETURN.
IT IS CALLED SQUID NO CROW.'

'You mean *quid pro quo*?'

No, it is definitely *squid no crow*. It refers to
the time six months ago when the Boss threw
out some leftover squid, and my aunts snatched
it all up, and Rufus said he would never crow
again unless they gave him some of it.

But I don't bother explaining this to Olive.
A team only needs one real detective. I will
lead, and she will follow. I will think, and she
will do my bidding.

I wait till she's asleep, then make a list.

1. Someone is stealing the valuable sheep.

2. Who steals things? Master criminals.

3. Who are master criminals? They are nasty
   people.

4. Who is a nasty person? Jubilee Crystal
   Simpson.

5. Therefore, Jubilee Crystal Simpson is
   stealing the valuable sheep!

This is called scientific thinking, and I am very good at it. Olive is not, but she will learn.

For now, however, I keep my reasoning to myself. I must find proof. Then, like Amelia X in Episode 8, I will line everyone up in the library and tell them how I have solved the crime.

(Note to self: find a library.)

Thursday

~~Dear Mum~~

~~Dear diary~~

~~Dear anyone~~

Dear Mum, is it weird, me writing to you? It feels weird but it's kind of comforting too. As if you might actually read it. As if you might write back.

Mrs

Sorry, that bit got smudged. Auntie Gina says I should cry as much as I want to, and no one's going to judge me for it. But *I* judge me. You've been gone for almost a year and I'm sick of crying. Mrs Savage says the human body is made up of 60% water, and I reckon I've cried a good 58% of it. Maybe when that last 2% is gone, I'll just float away like a cloud.

Except then Dad would be left by himself, and that wouldn't be fair. (He cries too, though he pretends he doesn't.)

Mrs Savage gave me another poem today. She slipped it into my hand as I was leaving, so no one else would see. This one's by a man called Billy Collins, and it's about dead pe

Sorry, more smudges

It's about dead people rowing themselves across heaven in glass-bottomed boats, and looking down on us while we're making a sandwich or putting on our shoes.

I hope – I really hope you've got a glass-bottomed boat, Mum. It's exactly the sort of thing you'd like. And if you have, then you already know about Clara, who is sweet, and slightly ~~mad~~.

I AM NOT A DUCK. See what I mean? Ha ha ha. (No, that wasn't a proper laugh. I think I've forgotten how.)

I don't know what I'm going to write to you about. Maybe the stock theft thing. Last night, I wasn't sure about helping Dad – not because I didn't want to, but because I didn't really believe we could do anything. And besides, it'd mean I'd have to talk to people, which is kind of hard at the moment.

But now I think we *have* to help him. Because I'm not leaving here, Mum. You loved Little Dismal, and so does Dad and so do I. And if you truly have got a glass-bottomed boat, it'll be right above us somewhere. And if we moved, you might not be able to find

Smudges. Sorry.

Lots of love from Olive

Friday

Dear Mum, this morning before school, Clara announced that she wants to stake out Jubilee Simpson's secret hide-out. I think she's got visions of a raid, or maybe a shootout. She's obsessed with Jubilee, so I don't think she's going to be much help with the stock thefts. But it's kind of nice having her around.

Anyway, I explained (again) that it can't be Jubilee, and that we need to do some research to find out what people already know about the thefts. And since Dad's the local policeman, he's the obvious person to ask, right?

Ha ha. (That wasn't a proper laugh either.)

You know how you used to say that Dad and I are really alike? Well, I think that's part of the problem. Neither of us were very good at talking about stuff even before you got sick. But now we're even worse. Talking just feels like a big waste of time when I could be doing something much better. Like lying in bed with the doona over my head.

Don't worry, I don't do that all the time, especially not now Clara's here. Would you believe she wakes me up at half past five??? This morning she started teaching me semaphore – you've never seen anything like it, Mum. It was the weirdest thing I've ever done, but it was kind of fun, with her waving her wings around and me trying to copy her (with my arms, not my wings).

And that's weird, too. Me saying something was fun, I mean. I'd kind of forgotten about fun.

Sorry about the smudges. I think I'd better stop apologising for them, or I'll spend my whole time saying sorry.

After semaphore training Clara headed out to the garden, and a bit later I heard that excited clucking sound that chooks make when they've just laid an egg. So I went looking for it, but I couldn't find it. I'll try again tomorrow. I'd love an egg for breakfast – anything would be better than baked beans.

I know Dad's really busy. But he used to like cooking. I guess that's just one of the things that's changed.

Anyway, our usual breakfast conversation goes something like this:

Dad: grunt (meaning, 'How are you this morning, Olive?')

Me: grunt grunt (meaning, 'Pretty horrible, thanks for asking. How are *you*?')

Dad: grunt grunt (meaning, 'Equally horrible. Have a nice day at school.')

Me: grunt grunt (meaning, 'School's horrible. Have a nice day at work.')

Dad: grunt (meaning, 'Work's horrible too'.)

But this morning I was determined to get some information out of him. So I sat down beside him and said, 'Dad, what's happening with the stock thefts?'

He was working on his laptop while he ate. 'Have you told Gina about that chook of yours yet?' he asked.

'Not yet. So, have you got any idea who's behind the thefts?'

'Tell her,' said Dad. 'Right now.'

He wouldn't budge, so I phoned Auntie Gina, and she said Clara could stay for a while and it'd do her good to get away from the other chooks. But unlike Dad and me, Auntie Gina doesn't have any trouble talking, and she wanted me to visit her after school. She wouldn't take no for an answer, and by the time I hung up, Dad had finished his breakfast and gone to work.

So that was a waste of time.

You know how in books they have a little row of stars or something to show time passing?

These are for you in your glass-bottomed boat.

After school I rode out to Auntie Gina's farm. I thought Clara would want to go with me, but when I asked her she went all small and scared. I hadn't seen her like that before, and it was horrible. I think it was because of the other chooks.

I almost said, 'Do you want to talk about it?' But then I remembered how much I hate people saying that to me. So instead, we pretended she was too busy to come.

Auntie Gina had made scones, and I ate six of them. She gave me another six wrapped up in a tea towel to take home for Dad, but he probably won't eat them. He's gone all stubborn, Mum. He won't accept help from anyone, including family. If you were here, you could talk him out of it, but I don't even know where to start.

If you

Sorry, smudge.

While I was at Auntie Gina's, I asked her about the stock thefts. She told me who'd lost sheep, and said the whole thing started back in November, as far as anyone can tell. That's part of the problem – because the farms are so spread out, people often don't realise some of their sheep are missing for a week or more.

'By then the thieves are long gone,' she said. 'And so are any tyre tracks or any other sort of evidence, which makes it really hard for your dad.'

'Do you think he'll catch the thieves?' I asked her.

I wanted her to say, 'Yes, of course he will.' He needs people to believe in him, Mum.

But Auntie Gina just looked worried. 'I hope so, Olive. Farmers are doing it hard enough without this on top of everything else.

Maybe something good will come out of the meeting tomorrow.'

And that's when I learned that there's a meeting after the footy match tomorrow, to talk about the thefts! Auntie Gina said no one's quite sure who called it, but I don't think it was Dad. It's not the sort of thing he'd do. I'm not sure he even knows about it. I certainly didn't.

Love, Olive

Saturday

5.30 AM

I fly down from the wardrobe rail and prepare for First Squawk, but Olive rolls over, grabs my beak and mumbles, 'No, Clara. Please?'

I can't begin the day without First Squawk. But a good detective must learn to compromise, especially with her sidekick. I wait until she has her hands over her ears, then I do it very quietly.

5.45 AM

Semaphore practice. We get to the end of the alphabet and start again. Olive is a quick learner.

6.15 AM

I have been thinking about the three rules of the chookyard. Olive is gradually improving with regard to Rule #1 (Get Up Early So You Don't Miss Out), but she and Constable Dad are not doing at all well on Rules #2 and #3 (Keep A Clean House So As Not To Attract Rats, and A Varied Diet Is A Healthy Diet).

It is time I stepped in. While Olive gets dressed, I head for the kitchen sink.

I eat the leftovers off the dinner plates, then fly down to perch on the edge of the overflowing rubbish bin. It tips over and all the rubbish spills out onto the floor, which makes it nice and easy to search for food.

Rats aren't interested in empty tins, plastic bags and suchlike, so I kick them out of the way and get on with

the job. By the time I've finished, there's not a single bean, scone or bit of toast left in the rubbish.

Satisfied that I have done my duty, I hop carefully around the empty tins and plastic bags, and go outside to the compost heap. As I begin Worm Hunt, I hear Olive shriek, 'Clara, what have you *done*?'

She's obviously impressed with my cleaning.

7.00 AM

Egg O'Clock. I stroll across the backyard towards my comfortable nest under the bush, murmuring quietly to myself. I duck under the bush—

And stop in shock. The nest is empty. The eggs I laid yesterday and the day before and the day before that aren't there!

I search all around the nest, in case they've rolled out. I turn over the leaves. I poke my head under the bush next door, in case

I've gotten turned around somehow and was looking in the wrong place.

But my eggs are gone.

No, not gone. The Boss is the only one who collects eggs, and she is not here. So they must have been stolen.

Now I have two mysteries – the stock thefts and the missing eggs. Are they connected? Are they both the work of Jubilee Crystal Simpson, master criminal? Or is there a sneaky rat nearby?

These are not the sort of eggs that will hatch out into chicks, but I still don't want a rat to have them.

There's no time to investigate, however, not with another egg on its way. I leave my old nest behind and make a new one behind the compost heap on the other side of the yard. Then I sit and think about yesterday.

When Olive asked me to go to the farm with her, I found myself huddling down as if Rufus and the other chooks were looming over me with their fierce eyes and their sharp beaks. I forgot I was a detective. I pretended I was too busy to go with her.

Inspector Garcia *never* pretends she is too busy. I have let my sidekick down.

Today I will make up for it.

7.30 AM

Olive has cleaned up all the not-very-interesting rubbish that was on the floor and in the bin, and put it outside. Now she's cooking something called an omelette.

When it's done, she cuts it and gives half to herself and half to Constable Dad. It is a beautiful shade of yellow.

Constable Dad looks surprised, but he eats it and says, 'That was – nice.'

Olive seems a little happier than she was yesterday. She finishes her breakfast and says, 'Thanks, Clara.'

I'm not sure what she's thanking me for. Probably for letting her be my sidekick. *'You're welcome,'* I squawk.

9.30 AM

Olive gets a map and shows me the farms where sheep have gone missing. She has done quite well for a sidekick, but I am way ahead of her.

'WILL JUBILEE CRYSTAL SIMPSON BE AT SCHOOL TODAY?' I ask.

'No,' says Olive, 'it's Saturday. There's no school on Saturday.'

'THEN WE MUST FIND HER SECRET HIDE-OUT AND SET UP AN OBSERVATION POST.'

'She hasn't got a secret hide-out, Clara. She lives at the pub with her dad.'

'THAT'S HER HEADQUARTERS? THEN WE WILL SET UP AN OBSERVATION POST OPPOSITE THE PUB.'

'Look, Clara.' Olive takes a deep breath. 'It's not Jubilee, okay? If you want to help Dad, you have to accept that.'

'WHO LIVES OPPOSITE THE PUB? PLEASE ARRANGE FOR US TO USE THEIR UPSTAIRS ROOM.'

'It's not Jubilee!'

'DO YOU HAVE BINOCULARS? AND A WALKIE-TALKIE?'

'No, I don't. And if I did, I wouldn't give them to you.'

I write, 'YOU ARE NOT A VERY GOOD SIDEKICK.'

'And you're not a very good detective,' she snaps.

We glare at each other. I walk away.

10.00 AM

I do not need a sidekick. I did perfectly well without one back at the farm, when I solved the Mystery of the Missing Eggs, and I will do perfectly well without one now. Sidekicks are useful, but not necessary.

And some sidekicks are not even useful.

Thanks to Inspector Garcia, I know exactly how to set up an observation post by myself. I may not have binoculars or a walkie-talkie, but my eyesight is excellent and, if necessary, I can squawk very loudly.

I set off for town, and Jubilee Crystal Simpson's headquarters.

10.15 AM

I'm halfway to town when Olive catches up with me on her bike. 'Clara,' she says, skidding to a halt, 'I'm sorry, I didn't mean it.'

I keep walking.

Olive hops off her bike and walks beside me. 'Really I didn't,' she says. 'Please come back.'

I keep walking.

'You're a *good* detective,' she says. 'But you're wrong about Jubilee.'

I keep walking.

Olive rolls her eyes. 'Look, she won't even be at home this afternoon. She'll be at the footy, like everyone else. By the time you finish setting up the – um – observation post, she'll be gone.'

I stop, and semaphore, 'WHAT IS FOOTY?'

'That was a W, wasn't it?' says Olive. 'And an I? Or was it an H? Sorry, could you write it down?'

She puts her phone on the ground beside me, and I write the question again. 'WHAT IS FOOTY?'

'Football,' says Olive. 'It's a game. Little Dismal's playing Yabby Creek.'

'AND JUBILEE CRYSTAL SIMPSON WILL BE THERE?'

Olive nods. 'She reckons it's not nearly as good as American football, and the rules are dumb and the umpiring is weird blah blah blah. But she still goes to watch every week.'

'TAKE ME THERE.'

'What? No, I haven't been to the footy since – since ages.'

'TAKE ME THERE.'

'I said no, Clara. I don't want to. There are too many people, and some of them—'

'TAKE ME THERE.'

'But I—'

'TAKE ME—'

Olive snatches the phone from under my beak. 'All right, you don't have to keep saying it. We'll go to the footy!'

Saturday

2.00 PM

When Olive sees all the people standing around talking at the footy she goes small, like I did yesterday.

Most of the people smile or wave, and she doesn't seem to mind those ones so much. But two women hurry over to talk to her. 'Olive,' says one of the women, tipping her head to one side and looking sorrowful. 'You poooor dear thing, we've been thinking about you and your poooor father. How are you getting on?'

'Fine thanks, Mrs Fullerton,' mumbles Olive.

'Is there anything we can do to help?'

asks the other woman. 'Anything at all? You know you just have to ask.'

'We're fine. Um – thanks, Mrs Briggs.'

'We were so fond of your poooor dear mother,' says Mrs Fullerton. 'What a lovely woman she was, and what a loss to Little Dismal. You must be heartbroken. We were just saying to each other the other day, poooor Olive must be heartbroken.'

Olive stares at the ground.

'And is this your pet chook?' asks Mrs Briggs. 'What a sweet little thing she is. I'm sure she's a great comfort—'

A hand stretches out towards me. I'm just about to peck it, as hard as I can, when a voice somewhere behind us cries, 'Hey, Olive. Over here!'

With a gasp of relief, Olive mumbles, 'Sorry, I have to go.' And she runs away to where Digby is sitting on a railing.

'Thought you might need rescuing,'

he whispers when Olive and I sit down next to him. 'Aren't they awful?'

'Horrible,' whispers Olive.

Digby nods towards me. 'Isn't that Clara? What's she doing here?'

'The other chooks were being nasty to her, so she's come to me for a break,' says Olive.

'Good idea,' says Digby, and he offers Olive some hot chips. 'Clara,' he says, 'would you like some too?'

The three of us perch on the railing, eating chips and watching some humans chase a ball up and down the field. Olive is quiet, but Digby cheers and shouts, 'Go, Little Dismal!'

Go where? And why? I can understand them chasing the ball, because chasing things is fun. But when they catch it, they *don't eat it*!

Humans are strange.

2.15 PM

I thought Olive understood why we were here,

but she seems content to sit next to Digby and do nothing at all about Jubilee Crystal Simpson. I try semaphore, but she looks the other way. I try to get her phone out of her pocket so I can give her instructions, but she pushes it deeper.

I'm sure Inspector Garcia never had this sort of trouble.

In the end I have no choice. I set off between the cars and people, searching for Jubilee Crystal Simpson, master criminal. I will do the stake-out myself.

2.30 PM

I find my quarry perched on the bonnet of a yellow car, next to Tracy.

I know all about cars. Some of them are shiny and obedient, and others are old and cranky, and you have to talk to them to make them go anywhere. The Boss's car is *very* cranky. 'Don't let me down, old girl,' she says, when she wants it to carry her to town. 'Start nicely, now. That's it, that's the way. Good girl!'

The yellow car isn't *that* old, but it's not new and shiny either. A man is sitting beside it on a folding chair. His Merrycan accent tells me that he is Mr Simpson, Jubilee's father.

I wonder if he knows about his daughter's life of crime.

There's a white car next to the yellow one, and I speak to it politely. 'Excuse me, car, do you mind if I use you for an observation post?'

The car says nothing, so I creep under it and take a position next to one of its wheels. Then I fix my eye on Jubilee, and wait for her to do something illegal.

2.45 PM
Still waiting.

3.00 PM
Still waiting. Inspector Garcia's stake-outs

usually involve hamburgers, but I don't have any, so I catch grasshoppers instead.

3.15 PM

When Inspector Garcia does a stake-out, her targets always meet up with someone they shouldn't, or hide large amounts of cash in a rubbish bin, or dispose of a body. Jubilee Crystal Simpson just sits on the bonnet of the car, talking to Tracy and looking at her phone.

Shouldn't a master criminal be more interesting than this?

4.30 PM

At last something is happening. A siren blows. Everyone cheers. Mr Simpson folds up his chair and puts it in the boot of the yellow car.

As Tracy walks away, Jubilee hops down from the bonnet – just as the car above my head suddenly roars at me.

I dash out from underneath it, straight across Jubilee's path. She stumbles and nearly falls. 'You stupid chook!' she cries.

No one else seems to hear her over the roar of the car. So I am probably the only one who wonders why, for those three words, she had no Merrycan accent at all.

Saturday night

Dear Mum, the meeting about the stock thefts was kind of good and kind of bad at the same time.

It was held straight after the footy match, so everyone was in town and the hall was crowded. Digby and I sat up the back, with Clara hiding in my schoolbag. (Well, she said she was hiding. I think she was asleep.)

We still didn't know who'd called the meeting, so it was a big surprise when Mr Simpson marched up the front and climbed onto the stage. (He bought the pub three months ago, and he's one of those jolly people who everyone likes.

I have no idea how he had a horrible daughter like Jubilee.)

A couple of people cheered him, but most of us just shut up, waiting to hear what he had to say. There was no sign of Dad.

'I want to start by thanking you good folks for coming here today,' Mr Simpson said in a loud voice. 'I hope you know by now that I don't like to put myself forward. There's nothing special about me. I'm just a humble feller who happened to make a bit of money, that's all.'

Shorty Davis shouted from the other side of the hall, 'You're a good bloke, Ernie. We'd have lost the pub if you hadn't bought it.'

One of his friends yelled, 'Where would you've spent your days then, Shorty?'

'He might've had to get a job,' shouted someone else.

Everyone laughed, but they quietened down really quickly, wanting to know what Mr Simpson had to say next.

'Now I grew up in a small farming community myself, even if it was on the other side of the Pacific Ocean,' he said. 'So I know what it's like to do it tough. And I know that everyone in a place like this helps out, even newcomers like me and my daughter. That's why I called this meeting. Because I want to help and I'm in a good position to do so.'

The people in front of me were glancing at each other, trying to work out what he was building up to.

'But first,' said Mr Simpson, 'let's have a big round of applause for Constable Dave Hennessey. I know he's trying his hardest to catch the lowlife scum who've been stealing sheep, but there's only so much one man can do. Dave, this is for you.'

He started to clap, and everyone joined in. But at the same time they were peering around the hall as if they were wondering why Dad wasn't there.

'So let's get down to business,' Mr Simpson

said, when the clapping died away. 'I'm trying to source some CCTV cameras for the more remote corners of our great little community. I want to give Dave Hennessey a hand, and get those sheep-stealing scum on film.'

Everyone started talking at once. Shorty Davis called out, 'How much will the cameras cost?'

'Don't you worry about the cost,' said Mr Simpson. 'That's my contribution.'

When they heard that, everyone clapped again. Someone yelled, 'Three cheers for Ernie!'

But Mr Simpson was raising his hands for quiet. 'There's something else. The cameras won't come straight away, and in the meantime I think we should set up a roster for watching the roads at night. I know you all work hard during the day, and the last thing you want to do is go out again. But Dave Hennessey can't be everywhere at once – and I'll be the first one to put my name down. Who's with me on this?'

The rest of what he said was drowned out

by the sound of cheering. It went on for ages, and as soon as it stopped, people started making suggestions as to where the cameras might go, and who'd be on the roster.

Digby and I sat watching for a few minutes more. Then we left, with Clara still in my schoolbag.

As we walked out the door, I heard Mrs Briggs say, 'Why hasn't Constable Hennessey bought CCTV cameras and set up a roster? He's the policeman. He's the one with all the resources. It shouldn't be left to Ernie Simpson to do it.'

Yes, I know these aren't stars. I don't feel like stars.

Love, Olive

Sunday

5.30 AM

First Squawk. Olive groans, but rolls out of bed without complaining.

5.45 AM

Semaphore practice. Olive spells out 'R-E-S-U-E-R'.

'Hang on,' she says. 'I don't think that was right.' She tries again. 'R-O-S-T-E-R.' She smiles. 'I think I'm starting to get it,' she says.

I have forgiven her for not helping me yesterday. It is not her fault if she does not see the bigger picture.

7.15 AM

Egg O'Clock. After a pleasant scratch in the garden, I wander over to my new nest behind the compost heap – only to find that yesterday's egg has disappeared!

I haven't seen Jubilee Crystal Simpson anywhere near the back garden, so it must have been a rat.

Quickly, I make a new nest in the long grass beside the garage, and settle down to think about yesterday's investigation. I must remember to tell Olive about Jubilee Crystal Simpson's missing accent. It is a clue. An important one.

7.40 AM

Olive is in the kitchen cooking an interesting-looking white thing with a round yellow blob in the middle in a frying pan. I'm about to ask her if she saw the rat that took my egg, when she looks up and says, 'Thanks, Clara.'

She thanked me yesterday morning, and now she is thanking me again. Is this some strange human ritual that I didn't know about?

8.30 AM

While Olive is out of the room, her phone buzzes. I approach it cautiously. Is there an insect trapped inside? A bee? (Bees are crunchy.) A wasp? (Wasps are nearly as nasty as rats.)

I tap the edge of the phone with my beak. *'Hello?'* I say.

It buzzes again. It does not sound like a wasp.

I look at the screen – and there is a message. Someone inside the phone is sending messages to Olive!

The message says, 'u r ugly an stupid everywun hates u'.

The person inside the phone cannot spell. I wonder if it is a very small duck. Ducks are dreadfully bad at spelling.

The only way to find out is to ask. 'ARE YOU A DUCK?' I write.

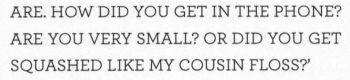

Another buzz. Maybe it's a duck *and* a bee.

'u r mad,' says the message.

'I AM NOT A DUCK, YOU ARE. HOW DID YOU GET IN THE PHONE? ARE YOU VERY SMALL? OR DID YOU GET SQUASHED LIKE MY COUSIN FLOSS?'

'u r mad'

'IT IS NOT GOOD MANNERS TO SAY THE SAME THING TWICE. BUT A DUCK WOULD NOT UNDERSTAND GOOD MANNERS.'

The phone buzzes again, just as Olive comes into the room.

'u r stupid'

Olive gasps. 'Has she sent another message? You didn't answer it, did you? I never answer her messages, it just encourages her.'

122

Her? It is a she-duck?

Olive snatches up the phone and reads the conversation. She puts her hand over her mouth. She smiles. 'Oh,' she says. 'That's really funny.'

I do not understand what is so funny about my conversation with the duck.

'WHO WAS IT?' I write.

'Jubilee Crystal Simpson,' says Olive, pulling a face.

I stare at her. The master criminal is *inside Olive's phone?*

'HOW DID SHE GET IN?'

'What do you mean?'

'HOW DID SHE GET IN THE PHONE? AND HOW DO WE GET HER OUT?'

Olive bites her lip. 'She's not in the phone, Clara. She's sending me a message from *her* phone. I can't prove it's her, but I know it is. She's been doing it for weeks. I try to ignore it, but it's pretty horrible.

Her face brightens. 'But I never thought of writing nonsense back to her. That was a really good idea.'

I have no idea what she is talking about. Who is writing nonsense?

Sunday night

Dear Mum, Clara is the cleverest chook in the world, but like I told you, she's got this obsession about Jubilee Simpson. So yesterday, while Digby and I were watching the football, she went spying.

I'm not sure what happened, but now she's got it into her head that Jubilee's American accent is fake.

I didn't want to bother Dad about it, because Clara gets so many things wrong, and I was sure she'd got this one wrong too. But she kept writing 'IT'S A CLUE. TELL HIM' on my phone, and then semaphoring the same words. So I thought I could at least check in a roundabout sort of way, just to show her it wasn't true.

Dad was working at the kitchen table this morning, with his laptop, maps and notebooks spread out in front of him. I sat down, and Clara perched on the back of my chair.

'Why don't you have a friend over?' he said, without looking up from his notebooks. 'What about Tracy? You two used to be good mates.'

'You arrested her uncle for selling drugs, Dad! It's kind of hard to be good mates after that.'

'Oh. Right. Well, what about Digby?'

'I don't want to have a friend over. I want you to tell me about the stock thefts.'

He shook his head.

'Why not?' I asked him.

'Because I don't want you worrying about it.'

'*Pleeeeease*, Dad,' I said.

Mum, remember how he used to come home from work and tell you about his day? And then you'd tell him about your day? And you'd both kind of relax as you did it, as if you were putting down a heavy load?

He didn't do that exactly, but he gave in pretty easily.

'There's a pattern,' he said. 'I've been in touch with a couple of coppers in New South Wales where the same thing happened. The thefts went on for six months or so, then stopped, and the culprits were never caught. One of the blokes I spoke to had a description of a truck that was spotted driving at night without any lights. But he couldn't give me anything more definite.'

He flipped through the pages of his notebook, then glanced up at me. 'You know you can't tell anyone about this?'

'Cross my heart,' I said.

'I've been trying to trace ear tags,' he said, 'to see where the stolen sheep went. But I've also been checking backgrounds. People who might've been up in New South Wales last year. People who've moved here recently.'

'The Simpsons,' I breathed. And for one amazing moment, I thought that maybe Clara was right after all. And I was really pleased, because I hate Jubilee so much, and also because Dad and I were having a proper conversation for the first time in ages.

But then he said, 'The Simpsons were certainly on my list, along with the Wyatts and the Aboods. But I've checked them all out, and they're who they say they are. Not a hint of suspicion about any of them.'

See, Mum, he was way ahead of Clara. She'd got it wrong, just as I thought.

Except she didn't want to believe it. She flew from the back of my chair onto the table and started scratching at Dad's precious notebooks. She tore one of them almost in half before I could grab her, and Dad was furious. He yelled at me to keep my chook out of the house, and I yelled back, because we were just trying to help.

And that's how Dad and I ended up not talking to each other *at all.*

We miss you, Mum. We miss you so much.

Love, Olive

Monday

5.30 AM

First Squawk. Olive shouts at me to go away, then burrows under the blankets. She has obviously forgotten the first rule of the chookyard.

5.45 AM

Olive refuses to join in semaphore practice, so I do it myself, standing on the lump that is her head and squawking the letters as loudly as I can.

6.20 AM

On the farm, Grandmother Polly sometimes

decides that Scratch O'Clock will come *before* Egg O'Clock instead of after. No one else is allowed to make this announcement, not even Rufus.

But Grandmother Polly is not here.

'It is now Scratch O'Clock,' I say to Olive's blankets. And I trot out to the compost heap and take out my annoyance on the earwigs. But as I gobble them down, with worms and spiders for dessert, I am struck by inspiration.

Why are Constable Dad and Olive so bad-tempered? Because of their *diet*! It isn't varied enough. It isn't healthy enough. All those beans would make anyone cross.

Luckily for them, I am here to help. I leave the rest of the worms for tomorrow and hurry around the back of the garage, where I spotted several mice yesterday.

7.30 AM

Egg O'Clock. Yesterday's egg is missing, so I can't use the same nest again. But this time I will fool the rat thief! I will lay my egg in the house, where the thief will never think to look.

I gallop through the kitchen just as Constable Dad stumbles in. I'm making myself comfortable in the bottom of Olive's wardrobe when I hear him bellow, 'Why is there a dead mouse on my plate?'

He has found my gift. I hope he realises what a sacrifice it was on my part. I could have eaten it myself, but his need was greater.

In the kitchen, Olive shouts, 'It wasn't me!'

'No, it was your chook,' roars Constable Dad, 'and I've had enough. First she tears up my notebook, then she brings vermin into the house. She has to go!'

'She's not going anywhere,' shouts Olive. 'And she probably *didn't* bring it into the house, it was probably already here because you never do any cleaning and I can't do it all myself and the house is probably *full* of mice and – and vermin, and you don't even *care!*'

They are obviously enjoying themselves. I snuggle deeper into the wardrobe and focus on my egg.

7.45 AM

The egg comes slowly, which gives me plenty of time to think. Olive refuses to believe that Jubilee Crystal Simpson is behind the stock thefts, and so does Constable Dad. A varied diet is not enough to change their minds. I need proof.

Inspector Garcia always gets to the crime scene minutes after it happens, so she can collect evidence. If I am to bring Jubilee Crystal Simpson to justice, I must do the same.

8.15 AM

'What do you mean, roosters?' asks Olive. She's

getting ready for school, slamming books into her bag and stamping around her bedroom.

'WE NEED SOMEONE TO WATCH THE ROADS AT NIGHT,' I write.

'They've set up a roster to watch the roads, Clara. And Mr Simpson's getting cameras, and Dad is doing policeman stuff, which is obviously way more important than anything to do with his daughter, and I don't know why we bothered to try and help him, because he doesn't *want* our help. In fact, he probably doesn't want anything to do with us. He probably wishes he didn't have a daughter, so he could stay at his stupid police station all night and never come home, and then he wouldn't have to worry about stupid things like cleaning.' She slams another book into her bag.

She is angry with Constable Dad. I don't blame her – if I'd known he wasn't going to eat the mouse I would've eaten it myself. But we must not lose sight of what's important.

'WE NEED OUR OWN WATCHERS,' I write. 'WE SHOULD ASK THE ROOSTERS.'

Olive stares at me as if I was a duck.

So I explain. 'ROOSTERS ALWAYS WANT TO KNOW WHAT IS HAPPENING. THEY WON'T CARE ABOUT SHEEP, BUT IF WE TELL THEM SOMEONE IN A TRUCK IS STEALING CHOOKS THEY WILL STAY UP ALL NIGHT WATCHING.'

Olive shakes her head. She laughs, but it is not a happy laugh. She picks up her schoolbag. 'If that's what you want to do, Clara, you do it. I have to go.'

'I WILL COME WITH YOU AND TRY IT OUT ON THE SCHOOL ROOSTER.'

8.35 AM

Olive is still in a bad mood, but I am not. Today I do not ride in the schoolbag. Today I ride on the handlebars with the wind in my feathers.

It is glorious.

8.50 AM

I hop off the bike just before we reach the playground, and Olive keeps going without me. *'I'll see you after school,'* I squawk.

She doesn't turn around.

9.00 AM

I go looking for the chookyard. I am a little worried about talking to a strange rooster, but I remind myself that I am a detective, just like Inspector Garcia.

She would not worry. She would stride in with confidence.

So that is what I will do.

9.05 AM

I stride in with confidence.

The rooster and fourteen hens chase me out again.

9.30 AM

I creep in, hoping they won't notice me straight away.

They do.

10.30 AM

I try to explain what I want from a safe distance.

They turn out to be very fast runners.

11.15 AM

I do not like the school chooks.

Monday night

Dear Mum, I got a real shock when I met up with Clara after school today. One of her feathers was broken, and there was blood on the back of her head, as if someone had pecked her.

She looked so small and unhappy that I picked her up and cuddled her. 'What happened, Clara? Are you all right?'

She didn't even squawk. And when I held my phone nice and close so she could reach it, she didn't have anything to say. She just squatted in my arms, a little ball of misery.

After a while, I said, 'Some people are just mean.'

No answer.

'Jubilee tried to get me into trouble again today,' I said. 'She hid her lunch in my schoolbag, but I saw her go into the locker room, so I sneaked in and threw her sandwiches out the window. I don't know why I've never done that before. I just didn't think of it. But this morning I was still mad with Dad, so I fought back.'

Still no answer. I was getting worried about her, Mum, so I said, 'I think it's a good idea about the roosters.' (I don't really. But I wanted to cheer her up.)

She raised her head at last and used her claw to pull my phone closer. 'IT WILL NOT WORK,' she wrote. 'I HAVE NO AUTHORITY. THEY WILL NOT LISTEN TO ME.'

That's when I had the most amazing idea.

When we got home, I dug out my box of Barbies. Clara peered at them, and wrote, 'WHY ARE THESE VERY SMALL HUMANS DEAD?'

'They're not dead,' I told her. 'They're dolls. I used to play with them.'

'WHAT IS PLAY?'

'Never mind,' I said, rummaging through the box.

Remember the Barbie police badge you made for me when I was little? It's just like Dad's badge and I used to wear it everywhere, including to bed.

I sat and looked at it for ages. I don't think I could have given it to anyone except Clara, and even that was really hard.

But she needed something nice to happen, and this was the only thing I could think of. So I threaded a ribbon through the clasp, and hung the badge

around her neck. Then I picked her up and carried her to the mirror.

'Look,' I said.

She wriggled until I put her down. She peered at the badge out of one eye. She peered at it out of the other. She fluffed her feathers and flapped her wings.

I think she liked it.

'Mum made a whole lot of badges,' I said. 'But this was my favourite.'

Clara was still admiring herself, so I grabbed my phone and took a photo of her. Then I sat her on my shoulder and took a selfie.

'Smile,' I said.

Click.

We both looked at the photo for a long time.

'Do you think I'm ugly?' I asked her.

'YES,' she wrote. 'YOU DO NOT HAVE ANY FEATHERS.'

I laughed.

'DO YOU THINK I AM UGLY?'

'No, you're nice.'

We looked at the photo for a bit longer.

'So do you reckon the badge will work?' I asked her. 'With the roosters, I mean? Do you reckon they'll listen to you? Will it be enough?'

That's when Clara came up with another idea. I'm going along with it, Mum, because it makes her happy.

Love, Olive

PS. Dad came home early and cleaned the kitchen! And then he did a load of washing and vacuumed the *whole house*. Then he hugged me and said, 'Sorry for being a rotten dad.' And I said, 'You're not!' and I hugged him back.

Smudges. But good ones, not sad ones.

Tuesday

5.30 AM

First Squawk. Olive joins in, then laughs.

5.45 AM

Semaphore practice. I am wearing my police badge. (It is still beautiful.)

6.25 AM

I'm worried about the school rooster. Will he take notice of my new authority? Will he listen? I can't afford to lose any more tail feathers.

7.45 AM

Yesterday's egg has disappeared from the nest in the wardrobe! For the first time since leaving the farm I miss Rufus.

But I must deal with this on my own, so I lay my egg under Olive's bed instead.

8.15 AM

We leave the house early, with me riding on the handlebars again. It is even better than yesterday, because today I have the police badge. *'Follow that car!'* I squawk. *'Arrest that man! Go go go!'*

But as we get close to the school, I fall silent. My legs feel small and weak. I look at the police badge, and it doesn't seem quite as shiny.

Olive stops the bike and I hop down.

'Wait, I'm coming with you,' she says.

She takes a roll of black-and-white tape from her schoolbag and wraps it around her handlebars. She puts a police hat on her head. It is a bit small, but it stays on.

'Mum made this, too,' she says. 'I had a whole police uniform when I was little.'

She pats the handlebars. 'Hop up. An important police chook doesn't walk. She rides.'

I hop back up onto the handlebars and Olive pedals towards the chookyard. When we're nearly there, I tuck the police badge under my wing so it is hidden.

Then I raise my head, fluff out my feathers, and prepare to confront the school rooster once again.

8.30 AM

Olive rides right into the middle of the chookyard and stops. Fourteen hens and a rooster raise their heads and stare at us.

I gulp. But the police badge under my wing feels strong and important, and the black-and-white tape beneath my feet makes it clear that this is Official Business.

I hop down from the bike and strut towards the rooster, who recognises me from yesterday. *'Stranger in the yard!'* he squawks. And he and his hens lower their heads, ready to chase me out again with maximum damage.

But before they can move, I lift my wing and the badge swings into position on my chest feathers.

'Police business,' I snap. *'Who's in charge here?'*

The rooster blinks at me. The other chooks raise their heads, puzzled.

'Well?' I say. (I am channelling Inspector Garcia in Episode 4, when she walked into the headquarters of the Bloody Hand gang with only her trusty driver for backup.) *'I haven't got all day. Who's in charge?'*

By now, the rooster has remembered how important he is. He struts forward, twice as big as me and far more beautiful.

'I am in charge,' he says. 'Who are you, and what is THAT?' He glares at Olive, who is waiting quietly on the bike.

'Don't you know an official police bicycle when you see one?' I say scornfully. 'The human is my trusty driver, and I am Inspector Clara.'

I don't give him time to think about it. 'I am investigating a series of chook thefts from nearby farms.'

'Chook thefts?' The feathers on the rooster's neck stand up in horror. 'Ladies!' he squawks, turning in a circle and flapping his wings. 'Come here, ladies. There are chook thieves around. Line up, line up, make sure everyone's present!'

When all the hens are lined up, he looks back at me. 'No one's missing. The thieves haven't been here.'

'I'm very glad to hear it,' I tell him. 'But they

MAY come here, and that is where I need your help. I am setting up a network of roosters to watch the roads at night. You must look out for a truck of some sort, probably not using its lights—'

The rooster interrupts me. *'But at night I'm asleep.'*

'And that is when the thieves will come,' I say. *'They would not dare face a fierce fellow like yourself during the day.'* (Even Inspector Garcia uses flattery sometimes.)

'They would not,' he agrees. *'But still, I need my sleep.'*

'For roosters who help us,' I tell him, *'there will be a badge.'*

His neck feathers stand up again, but this time it is interest. *'A police badge?'*

'You are not a police officer,' I remind him. *'You cannot have a police badge.'*

He sulks briefly, then says, *'A shiny badge?'*

'A VERY shiny badge.' I wave a wing at Olive,

who gets off her bike, takes something out of her schoolbag and brings it over.

'Here you are, guv,' she says.

I take the badge in my beak and dangle it in front of the rooster. The hens gather around us, murmuring with admiration.

It is not as beautiful as the police badge, but it is still very fine. The rooster lowers his head to put it on, but I jerk it away.

'*Do you agree to watch the road every night?*' I ask him.

'*I agree,*' he says, without taking his eye off the shiny badge.

'*What is your name?*'

'Spike.'

'*Do you agree to alert the rooster network if you see a truck driving with its lights off, Spike?*'

'*I agree.*' He shuffles his feet impatiently and edges closer to the badge.

'*And do you agree to pass on any important messages from the rooster network?*'

'Yes,' he says.

I hold the ribbon so he can put his head through the loop. The badge falls onto his chest, and the writing on it flashes in the morning sun.

BARBIE FIREFIGHTER.

Spike stands on his tiptoes and flaps his wings with pride. *'Look at my badge!'* he crows. *'Look at my shiny badge!'*

The hens gather around him squawking, *'So handsome!' 'So beautiful!' 'So brave!'*

I fly back up onto the official police bicycle handlebars, and Olive wheels us out the gate, making siren noises.

'WhooooooOOOOOOOOOooooooooh. WhoooooooOOOOOOOOOooooh.'

I am overcome with pride. Even Inspector Garcia's trusty driver doesn't do siren noises.

Tuesday night

Dear Mum, you should have seen Clara this morning. She was so bossy and important, and the whole thing worked brilliantly. We're going round some of the farms after school tomorrow and the next day to hand out more badges to the roosters.

I know that sounds crazy, and I know it won't work. But it keeps Clara happy, and I can't think of anything else we can do that might help Dad.

Back to this morning. I was wheeling my bike around to the front of the school, with Clara perched on the handlebars, when I heard two other bikes coming up behind me.

You guessed it. Tracy and Jubilee. Ugh.

They rode up beside me. 'Ooh, look,' said Tracy. 'Olive Hennessey's brought a chook to school. Ha ha, what a loser.'

'Don't be mean, Tracy,' said Jubilee. 'Poor Olive can't help it if she hasn't got any friends.'

'She thinks she's so clever,' said Tracy, 'because her dad's a cop. But he's a loser too. And a liar!'

'He *is*?' said Jubilee, pretending to be shocked. 'Why, if there's one thing I hate, it's dishonest policemen. We'd better go, Tracy, before we catch some awful disease.'

And they stood up on their pedals and sped away laughing.

I shouted after them, 'At least my chook has a kind heart!'

School wasn't too bad today. I actually answered a couple of questions, which made Mrs Savage nod approvingly at me.

I really like her, Mum. She's never once looked at me in that awful pitying way that some people do when they hear about you. She treats me as if I'm still a normal person, not some sad little freak who has to be wrapped up in cotton wool in case I break.

And she gives me poems, slips them into my hand when no one else is watching. I don't always understand them, but I read them anyway.

Do you think she gives anyone else poems? Maybe she does. Maybe she gives poems to everyone in the class, and everyone thinks they're the only one.

I wonder what sort of poem she'd give to Jubilee.

'Dear Jubilee, don't be so evil
or I will turn you into a weevil.'

Ha ha. If only.

Anyway, today the secret poem handover

happened just before recess. And right in the middle of it, I saw Jubilee sneaking into the locker room. Tracy was watching me, so I pretended I hadn't seen a thing. But I knew I'd better get in there before anyone else to see what she'd done. And undo it if I could.

Except Fate took a hand.

I'm not sure if I really heard the snapping sound, or if I made it up later. But let's say I heard it. Like this:

Snap! And Jubilee screamed.

I definitely heard that. We all did. Every single person in the class jumped to their feet and ran towards the locker room. Tracy was shouting, 'Jubilee! Jubilee!'

Mrs Savage was trying to push past us without actually trampling on any of us in the process (because teachers trampling on children is frowned on in Little Dismal). 'What is it?' she demanded. 'Who screamed? Jubilee, was that you? What happened?'

By then, Jubilee was standing in the middle of the locker room wailing and holding out her hand. 'She hurt me! Olive Hennessey hurt me!'

'What on earth are you talking about?' said Mrs Savage. 'Olive wasn't anywhere near you. She was with me.'

Jubilee wailed louder. 'She put a mouse trap in her schoolbag. She did it on purpose!'

Everyone stared at the mouse trap, which was lying on the floor next to Jubilee's feet.

Mrs Savage said, 'Olive? Do you know anything about this?'

I shook my head. 'No, Mrs Savage,' I said. Because I didn't *know* anything, not for sure. But I had my suspicions.

Fact #1. There wasn't a mouse trap in my bag when I left it in the locker room.

Fact #2. The locker room window was wide

open, so a magpie or a kookaburra or – just guessing wildly here – maybe even a chook could fly in from outside.

Fact #3. Mrs Savage sometimes puts mouse traps up on top of the lockers where that same magpie or kookaburra (or chook) might find them.

'She's lying,' cried Jubilee. Her fingers looked red and sore, where the mouse trap had caught her. 'Look what she did!'

Tracy put her arm around Jubilee's shoulders and glared at me. 'That was mean, Olive Hennessey.'

There was a buzz of agreement from a few of the other kids. But Digby said, 'Jubilee, if the mouse trap was in Olive's bag, how did it end up on your fingers?

'I was just—' Jubilee stopped.

'She was trying to help,' Tracy said quickly. 'She was worried Olive might have stolen something else, weren't you, Jubilee? You were going to put it back, so she wouldn't get into trouble.'

Mrs Savage narrowed her eyes. 'That's an interesting excuse, Jubilee and Tracy. Perhaps you and I should have a little talk at lunchtime. Meanwhile, I assume there are no more mouse traps? Good. Let's have an early recess. And just a reminder, children, to keep your hands out of other people's property.'

Everyone went to their bags. There was a little empty space around Jubilee and Tracy, as if no one wanted to go near them.

Hear that sound, Mum? That's me singing under my breath.

'Dear Jubilee, don't be so evil ...'

Love, Olive

PS. Clara and I watched *Amelia X.* It's really good!

Wednesday night

Dear Mum, today after school we went to the Koch farm, the Favrettos, the Talbots, the Waddles and the Riccardis. My legs feel as if they're falling off after so much pedalling.

But we're getting around the roosters, and they've all agreed to help. You should see how they strut once they get their badges. So far, they're proudly claiming to be a Barbie air hostess, a doctor, a paramedic, a pilot and a journalist.

Clara takes it very seriously. I try not to laugh. Tomorrow we go to the McAllisters, Digby and Auntie Gina.

Love, Olive

PS. Shorty Davis was rostered to watch Yabby Creek Road last night, and he got drunk and arrested Mrs Fullerton for acting suspiciously. Dad had to get up in the middle of the night to sort it out. I wish I'd seen it.

Dad says the roster is causing more trouble than it's worth.

Thursday

5.30 AM

First Squawk. Olive is getting very good at it.

5.45 AM

Semaphore practice. Olive spells R-O-O-S-T-E-R.

7.30 AM

Olive is cooking breakfast. I hop up onto the counter to watch, and she says, 'Took me a while to find your egg yesterday, Clara. I wish you'd lay them in the same place every day.'

She collected my egg? *Olive* is the rat thief?

I stare at the pan of water with the beautiful

yellow and white thing bubbling away in the middle.

Could this be *mine*?

I look around frantically for Olive's phone, but it's nowhere to be seen.

I raise my wings and spell out M-I-N-E? Then I point my toe at the pan of water.

Olive frowns. She copies my wing movements with her arms. 'That's an M, right? Is that an N? And an E?'

Her face clears. 'Mine! That's what you're asking? You mean the egg? Yes, of course it's yours. You lay the best eggs I've ever tasted, Clara. Look at the colour. Isn't it beautiful?'

I stand on tiptoes. I flap my wings. *'Hello, egg,'* I squawk. *'Hello, beautiful egg. Hello, MY beautiful egg.'*

7.35 AM

Constable Dad eats my egg. On toast. I watch every bite.

'Olive,' says Constable Dad, with his fork halfway to his mouth, 'why is Clara looking at me like that?'

'I don't know,' says Olive. 'She's a chook of mystery, and she has her own reasons.'

I fluff out my feathers. I murmur the words to myself so I won't forget them. *'I am a chook of mystery and I have my own reasons.'*

Then I go back to watching Constable Dad.

8.30 AM

Olive goes to school, and I am left alone. At first, I am happy. The sun is shining, I lay beautiful eggs, and the rooster network is almost complete.

But then the worry starts to creep in. This afternoon we're going to the farm. This afternoon, I must face Rufus and Grandmother Polly.

Just the thought of them is enough to make me lose a couple of feathers. I'm sure Rufus is much bigger and fiercer than any of the other roosters we've visited. And Grandmother Polly is even worse.

Perhaps we don't need to go to my old home at all. Perhaps we could leave it out.

11.00 AM

Even the earwigs in the compost heap are not enough to occupy me today. I find a sunny spot for Dust Bath, and try to comfort myself with thoughts of my beautiful egg.

It doesn't work.

3.30 PM

Olive comes home. I'm trying to be brave, so I don't tell her about my fears. The official police bicycle leaves the station, heading for the McAllister's farm and then Digby's.

4.30 PM

Digby's rooster is called Matey, and he gets

the second-best badge, which is for a Barbie astronaut.

We're about to slip away when Digby arrives home. 'Hi Olive,' he says. 'What are you doing?'

'Taking Clara sightseeing,' says Olive.

Digby laughs. 'You are so weird sometimes. In a good way. Can I come?'

'I suppose so,' says Olive. 'We're going to your nan's farm next.'

5.00 PM

As we head for my old home, I tell myself not to be nervous. After all, I am not alone. When I face my tormentors, I will have my trusty driver at my back.

But when we glide into the yard, the Boss is there, with Rufus and the other chooks pecking around her feet.

'Olive!' she says. 'And Digby and Clara! My three favourite people. Come in, come in, I've just made pikelets, and I've got some of last year's strawberry jam to go with them.'

Olive looks at me uncertainly. I want to go inside with her and Digby, and eat pikelets. I want to stay as far away from Rufus and Grandmother Polly as I can.

But I'm here on a mission, and I must not fail. So I let Olive and Digby go into the house without me.

Olive runs back out to whisper, 'Will you be all right by yourself?'

I raise my wings and signal, Y-E-S.

'Good luck,' says Olive, giving me the last badge. And she disappears again.

I turn back to the yard – and realise that every single chook is staring at me.

The muttering starts. *'It's Clara.'*

'Ugly Clara.'

'Ugly Clara who tells lies.' That's Rufus.

'Ugly Clara who lays ugly eggs.' Grandmother Polly.

'What will we do with her?'

'Peck her.'

'Peck her.'

'Peck her.'

'Peck her.'

'PECK HER!'

I almost turn tail and run, as I have done so many times before.

But I know now that my eggs are *not* ugly. They are beautiful. *I* am not beautiful, but I have a kind heart. What's more, I am a Chook of Mystery. I am a detective. And I am on a very important case.

So instead of running away, I march towards them. My legs tremble and my comb wobbles nervously, but I keep going. I let the police badge fall across my chest. I squawk, just as I did at the school, *'Who's in charge here?'*

That stops them in their tracks.

'What do you mean?' demands Rufus. His neck feathers are still standing up; I'm not out of danger yet. *'I'm in charge, and you know it.'*

'So am I,' squawks Grandmother Polly.

I pretend to ignore them. *'I am working with the police to catch a dangerous gang of chook thieves.'*

That sends everyone into a fluster. The hens squawk. Rufus bounces from foot to foot, crying, *'Where are they? Let me at them! Where are they?'*

When the noise dies down a little, I say, *'That's the problem, we don't know where they are. So we are looking for a brave rooster to act as our local sheriff. He would have to wear this.'*

I let the Barbie sheriff badge fall to the ground. It glints in the sun, and Rufus is transfixed. So are the hens. But this could still go either way.

'Of course if I cannot find such a rooster here,' I say, *'I will have to try somewhere else.'* And with that, I pick up the sheriff badge, turn my back on Rufus and march towards the gate.

Everyone comes tearing after me. *'Wait wait wait!'* cries Rufus, lowering his neck feathers to a more friendly position. *'No need to go elsewhere. I'll help. What do I have to do?'*

'He'll help,' squawks Grandmother Polly. *'Don't go away, Clara. He'll help.'*

I explain about the night watch, and Rufus agrees to everything. Any time he hesitates, Grandmother Polly agrees on his behalf.

I hold up the badge so he can slip his head through the ribbon. The sheriff badge falls into place on his red feathers.

It looks very fine.

Rufus thinks so too. He preens. He struts. He crows loudly and proudly.

I stroll to the back door of the house, accompanied by my aunts, sisters and cousins, who are all squawking at once.

'What's it like working with the police?'

'Where can we get a badge like yours?'

'When are you coming to visit us again?'

I slip into the house without answering a single question.

Friday night

Dear Mum, Dad went shopping! And then he cooked! He made spaghetti bolognaise and Clara went crazy over the spaghetti and chased it around her plate as if it was trying to get away.

Dad didn't say much, but he *smiled*, which was like a shower of rain after a long dry spell.

Maybe we'll be all right after all.

Love, Olive

Saturday night

Dear Mum, Clara keeps waking me up in the middle of the night to ask if I've heard a rooster crowing. Honestly, she's driving me crazy. She really believes the rooster network is going to work, which is good because it makes her happy, and bad because *she keeps waking me up in the middle of the night*.

Apart from that, things are okay. No, better than okay.

Auntie Mel brought round a casserole, which was enough to feed about forty-five people, and Dad let her in and actually thanked her for the casserole, instead of mumbling something about 'not needing any help' and slamming the door in her face.

The other really good news is that Auntie Mel was at the pub last night and Mr Simpson announced that the CCTV cameras are on their way. She said everyone cheered when they heard it, and Mr DeVries, who lost forty-three merinos a few weeks ago, stood on the bar and made a speech. Which was long-winded and boring, because *Mr DeVries*. But for once no one minded.

I think Dad's relieved about the cameras. He'd rather they were police cameras, but anything's better than nothing.

Lots and lots and lots of love, Olive

Monday

3.00 AM

I am jolted out of sleep by the sound of distant crowing.

It's not unusual to hear crowing at this time of night; roosters have a terrible sense of timing. But this is a very particular crow.

'Wake up wake up wake up! Message passed on from Matey! He saw the truck with no lights! Wake up wake up wake up!'

I'm so excited that I fall off my perch in the wardrobe and tumble to the floor. But I'm up again straight away, flapping onto the bed and squawking in Olive's ear.

'Wake up! The rooster network has sent a message!'

'Go away,' she mumbles, and she pulls the pillow over her head.

I burrow underneath it and peck her ear. She squawks and throws the pillow at me. 'I'm trying to sleep. Go away.'

But this is far more important than sleep. I keep pecking Olive's ear until at last she rolls over and glares at me. 'This had better be good,' she says.

I semaphore an urgent message, but she's too sleepy to understand it. So I hunt for her phone, drag it over to her and wait impatiently while she turns it on.

'THE THIEVES,' I write. 'DIGBY'S ROOSTER MATEY SAW A TRUCK WITHOUT LIGHTS. HE SENT A MESSAGE.'

Olive stares at the phone as if she's forgotten how to read. She sits up. She blinks and rubs her eyes. 'You mean it *worked*?'

'WE HAVE TO TELL CONSTABLE DAD. GET HIM OUT THERE STRAIGHT AWAY.'

'Right. Tell Dad. Tell him ...'

'TELL HIM YOU GOT A MESSAGE.'

Olive doesn't move.

'TELL HIM—'

She puts her hand over the screen and says, 'Clara, you're sure about this? You're not making it up? Or – or getting it wrong?'

I push her hand away and write, 'LISTEN.'

She listens, and hears the crowing. 'It could be any old rooster,' she says uncertainly.

'IT'S A MESSAGE. A TRUCK WITHOUT LIGHTS!!!'

'You really are sure—'

I have lost patience with her. Sidekicks are supposed to *trust* their detective, not question them over and over again. I hop off the bed and hurry towards Constable Dad's bedroom.

3.10 AM

Constable Dad is even harder to wake than Olive. He groans and moans and tells me to go away.

Then Olive arrives in her dressing-gown. 'Dad,' she says, 'I think there's been another stock theft.'

'What?' He sits bolt upright, staring at her. 'Where? I didn't hear the phone.'

'Someone – um – sent me a message. They saw a truck driving with its lights off on Wattle Hut Road, near the Carellas'.'

'Who was the message from?' asks Constable Dad, climbing out of bed.

'Um – someone called Matey.'

'Friend of yours? In your class?' Constable Dad doesn't wait for an answer. 'It might be nothing, but I'd better check. Put the jug on, will you?'

Put the jug on what? The table? The floor? He doesn't say. But Olive seems to understand what he means. By the time he's dressed in his uniform and strapping on his handcuffs, she's standing by the door with a mug of black tea.

'Thanks, poppet,' says Constable Dad, grabbing the tea. 'I don't know how long I'll be—'

'We're coming with you,' says Olive.

'No you're not. Go back to bed.'

'Three sets of eyes are better than one. We might see something you miss, Dad.'

Olive picks me up. 'Come on, we haven't got time to stand around arguing.'

3.25 AM

Night is strange. Night is full of darkness and threat, and little squeaking sounds that Olive and Constable Dad don't seem to hear.

I don't like the darkness and the threat. But if I wasn't in the middle of an investigation, I would hunt down those squeaking sounds to see if they were tasty.

We drive slowly along Wattle Hut Road with the car windows down and Olive shining a torch along fences and gates. Our eyes are peeled for signs of criminal activity.

'I hope this isn't a wild goose chase,' says Constable Dad.

I stare at him. Why would we be chasing wild geese at this time of night? They'd be asleep. And if they weren't asleep they'd be *very* dangerous. No one messes with geese, not even Rufus.

Once again, I am astonished at the ignorance of humans. Perhaps I should write a book explaining these things. What would I call it? *Don't Be a Goose*, perhaps? Or *Mad Duck, Bad Duck*? Or *How to Count Your Chickens Before They Hatch*?

I'm still thinking about book titles when Olive shouts, 'Dad, stop!'

The police car pulls up just past a gate. Constable Dad grabs the torch from Olive, and we all scramble out of the car.

There's a chain around the gate, and a padlock. But the chain has been cut, and dangles uselessly.

Constable Dad shines the torch on the ground and makes a hissing noise between his teeth. 'Fresh tyre marks. At last.'

He takes some photos, walking carefully around the outside of the tyre marks so as not to damage them. (Just like Inspector Garcia, when she found Half-Tongue Harry's footprints at the scene of the murder!)

Then he ushers us back to the car, saying, 'I'll take another look in the morning. But for now, we'd better wake Mel and tell her the bad news.'

I'm about to hop up into the car when I see something glinting in the headlights. It is small and round, like one of the buttons on Constable Dad's shirt.

I take a good look at it. Then I pick it up and give it to Olive.

'Dad,' she says, 'look what Clara found. Do you think it belongs to the thieves?'

Constable Dad takes a plastic bag out of the glove box and drops the button into it. 'Maybe. There's no mud on it, so it hasn't been here for long. Well done, Clara!'

I fluff out my feathers with pride. Then I squawk, *'Onwards, Constable. Our work tonight is not yet done.'*

3.45 AM

While Constable Dad bangs on the back door of the farmhouse, I go looking for Matey. I find him teetering on the fence, half asleep.

He hops down when he sees me. *'Was it them? Was it the thieves?'*

'It was,' I tell him, even though we are not yet completely sure.

'I frightened them off,' says Matey. And despite his tiredness, he struts and flaps his wings, so that the astronaut badge on his chest bounces. *'I chased them away.'*

'You did. Now tell me exactly what you saw.'

'A truck the colour of a pale egg,' says Matey. *'No lights. Two humans inside it.'*

'How big was the truck?'

Matey looks around the yard. His eyes fall on a tractor. *'Bigger than the noisy thing. Not as big as the shed.'*

'Could you see anything in the back of it?' I ask him.

'The back was closed up like a chookhouse at night.'

Over by the back door, Constable Dad is explaining about the gate. 'You'd better come and check on your sheep,' he says to Mel, who is Digby's mother. 'It might be a false alarm, but it doesn't look good.'

'Blast!' says Mel. 'I wish Tony wasn't away.'

(I know the meaning of the word 'blast' from Episode 6 of *Amelia X*, in which bank robbers were trying to break into a safe. But why is Digby's mother talking about explosives at a time like this? Does she want to blow up the stock thieves? Or is she afraid her sheep will explode?)

Olive hurries over to join me. She takes something out of her pocket and puts it on the ground. It's another badge, a silver bar with HERO written on it in red letters, and a red ribbon attached.

'This is for Matey,' whispers Olive. 'For being

such a bold, brave rooster, and helping the police.'

When he sees the badge, the tiredness vanishes from Matey's eyes. *'For me?'* he squawks.

'For you,' I say. *'Lower your head, Hero Matey.'* And I slip the ribbon around his neck.

The new badge clinks against the old one. Over by the house, Constable Dad and Digby's mother climb into the police car and drive away.

Monday morning
just before dawn

Dear Mum, I'm so tired I can hardly think, but I've got to tell you. The rooster plan worked! Clara is brilliant, and so are the roosters, and Dad's got tyre prints and a button, and with any luck we won't even need the CCTV cameras.

What's more, Clara and I have got an ally.

Dad and Auntie Mel had just gone off to check on the sheep when Digby came hurrying across the yard.

'Mum said you got a message, Olive, from someone who saw the truck. Who was it? What did they see?' He spotted Matey, who was admiring his badges. 'And why is my rooster wearing medals? Why is he even up at this time of night?'

Clara and I looked at each other. Matey went stumbling off to the chookhouse to catch up on his sleep.

Digby narrowed his eyes. 'What's going on?'

I know that Clara likes Digby. She told me once that he has excellent taste in TV programs. Now, she raised her wings and semaphored, 'T-E-L-L H-I-M.'

'Are you sure?' I asked.

'Am I sure what?' said Digby.

'I wasn't talking to you,' I said. 'I was talking to Clara.'

'Yeah, right.' Digby rolled his eyes.

Clara signalled again, 'T-E-L-L H-I-M.'

'Is she okay?' asked Digby. 'She hasn't got mad chook disease or anything, has she?'

'She's fine,' I said. Then I took a deep breath and said, 'Have you ever heard of the rooster network?'

I told him about the badges, and Clara's plan to have the roosters watch all the roads, and the early morning alarm from Matey.

'No way,' said Digby, laughing. He looked from me to Clara and back again. 'I mean, I know Clara's cute, but she's a *chook*. So what really happened?'

I put my phone on the ground next to Clara, folded my arms and shut my mouth.

Clara pecked out a message. 'THAT IS WHAT REALLY HAPPENED I AM NOT CUTE YOU WOULD NOT CALL INSPECTOR GARCIA CUTE'

Obviously she was in no mood for full stops.

Digby picked up the phone. He read the message and his mouth fell open. But it was me he questioned, not Clara. 'How did you do that? Did you train her?'

I didn't say a word. Clara scratched at Digby's foot until he put the phone down again.

'ASK ME A QUESTION,' she wrote.

'Okay, big joke,' said Digby. 'I'll play along.

Um – Clara, how many chooks has Nan got?'

'23'

He blinked. 'Oka-ay. But Olive, you could have known that. We were there just the other day; you could have counted them and – and given her a signal or something.'

'Then ask her something I don't know,' I said.

Digby thought for a moment, then said, 'Clara, what did you do when we were watching Episode 11 of *Amelia X*?'

I thought Clara would tell him, and then he'd have to believe us. Instead, she took a step away from the phone, and hunched her wings as if she was embarrassed. No message, nothing.

'See?' said Digby, smirking. 'So tell me again, Olive, who saw the truck?'

'What happened in Episode 11?' I asked him.

'There were these trained hawks,' said Digby, 'and they were attacking Amelia and Jock. And—'

Clara dived for the phone. 'I HID UNDER THE SOFA I DO NOT LIKE HAWKS'

'Of course you don't,' I said. 'No sensible chook likes hawks.' I turned back to Digby. 'Well?'

But he was still looking at Clara's message, and shaking his head. 'No way,' he whispered. 'No way!' He stared at Clara. 'You really understand everything I'm saying? You really … I'm not going mad?'

'YOU ARE NOT A DUCK, DIGBY.'

'What does that even mean?' he asked.

'She's got this thing about ducks,' I said. 'But listen, Digby, you're not allowed to tell anyone. Promise you won't.'

'I promise,' he whispered. 'On one condition. You're helping your dad, right? So I want to be in on it. I want to help too.'

'I'll have to consult with Clara.'

'Of course you will,' said Digby. He was shaking his head again, but he backed off a little way to give us some privacy.

I squatted down beside Clara. 'What do you reckon? He could be helpful.'

'I WOULD HAVE TWO SIDEKICKS INSTEAD OF ONE,' she wrote. 'AMELIA X ONLY HAS ONE. AND JOCK DOES NOT HAVE POPCORN.'

'So we let him help?'

'YES. BUT HE MUST LEARN SEMAPHORE. AND TELL HIM—'

That's when she passed on Matey's description of the truck. I was just telling Digby, when Dad and Auntie Mel came back.

'Mum?' called Digby, as the car door opened. 'Are the sheep all right?'

Auntie Mel shook her head and leaned back against the car seat. She looked very tired. 'The ram's gone, and twenty ewes.'

'Your *champion* ram?' I said.

'I'm afraid so,' said Auntie Mel. 'We looked everywhere and couldn't find him. Add that to the tyre tracks and the cut chain ... We were going to move them into the home paddock tomorrow, because of the thefts.'

She put her head in her hands, and Digby

hugged her. 'We'll get them back, Mum. Don't worry. And at least we've got a description of the truck.'

'We have?' said Dad, climbing out of the car with his notebook in his hand. 'When did that happen?'

'I – um – got another message,' I told him. 'It's a white truck – or whitish – with a closed-in back. Sounds as if it's about the same size as Mr Waddle's Isuzu. Two people in the front.'

Dad was making notes. 'Anything else?'

I shook my head. Dad turned to Auntie Mel. 'Who knew you were going to move them closer to the house? Did you talk to anyone about it?'

Clara took a step closer, as if she was determined not to miss the answer.

Auntie Mel rubbed her eyes. 'I probably mentioned it to a few people. It's just one of those things you talk about, you know? Everyone's worried about the thefts.' She looked at Dad. 'You don't think anyone local is involved?'

'I'm beginning to wonder,' he said. 'Which is why I want you to keep this to yourself for now. You too, Digby. And Olive. The description and the tyre tracks are the first real break I've had, and I don't want anyone knowing about them. In fact, I'd rather no one knows that *we* know the sheep are missing. Can I rely on you?'

We all nodded. At least, Digby and his mum and I did. Clara just sat there looking thoughtful.

Love, Olive

Monday

5.30 AM

First Squawk.

'Go away, Clara. We were up half the night, remember? I only just got back to bed.'

6.30 AM

'Mumble mumble mumble – I thought I told you to go away – mumble mumble mumble.'

7.30 AM

'Is it even a school day? Really? No, I'm not getting up. Stop biting my ear and go away.'

8.30 AM

'Mumble mumble – what's the time? *What?* I'm going to be late for school! Why didn't you wake me up?'

9.30 AM

Olive wouldn't take me to school with her today. So I walk into town instead, keen to see how Constable Dad is going with his part of the investigations.

When I get to the police station, he's on the phone.

'Did you get the photos I sent? Of the tyre tracks? What do you reckon?' He grabs his notebook and starts writing. 'Mm-hm. Mm-hm. That's what I thought. Ties in with the description. Late-model Isuzu? ... Yeah, I think so ... Yeah ... Yeah. Can you send me a list of registrations?'

I flap up onto his desk, hoping to hear the other side of the conversation. (There is no one inside the phone. Olive has explained it to me.)

'Hello, Clara,' whispers Constable Dad. 'What? No, not you, Maz. I was just talking to – uh – someone who came into the office … Yes, thanks for that. I owe you one.' And he puts down the phone.

I know what happens next. Constable Dad will receive a list of everyone in the state who has a white (or whitish) late-model Isuzu. He will cross out most of them because:

(a) they are ninety-nine years old and can't get out of their chair without help

(b) they are overseas

(c) they are in jail

(d) they are dead.

This will leave a shortlist of no more than ten people. It will quickly be revealed that seven of them have an unbreakable alibi for last night.

Which leaves three. (One of them will be Jubilee Crystal Simpson.)

Constable Dad will pick up his police hat, jam it on his head with a grim expression, and set out to question those three people.

The criminal will be the least likely one. (Jubilee Crystal Simpson – I could have told him that days ago.)

Or the criminal will turn out to be *none* of those three, and Constable Dad will have to go back to his original list. After some careful enquiries, he will discover that one of the dead people is *not really dead* (Jubilee Crystal Simpson).

So I'm perched on the desk, waiting for Constable Dad to receive the list.

Instead, he makes another phone call. 'Josh? You know those stock thefts you had last year? I just want to check the description of the vehicle ... Right ... Okay ... Definitely sounds like the same one ... Yeah, I'm still chasing background on a couple of them ... Rightio ... Yeah, I'll let you know.'

Excellent! Now he will have *two* lists, and can crosscheck them (and find that Jubilee Crystal Simpson is on both).

But he doesn't. The lists don't arrive, which is completely wrong. In *Death in the City*, they never take more than a few minutes.

I settle down on the corner of the desk to wait.

11.30 AM
Waiting.

2.00 PM
Still waiting.

3.30 PM
The lists have not yet arrived. What is wrong with these people? Don't they know how a proper police department is supposed to work?

6.30 PM

I complain to Olive.

'These things take time,' she says.

No they don't. I have watched every episode of *Death in the City*, even the one where the villain was disguised as a giant rooster (which I found very upsetting). I know that the lists always arrive a few minutes after Inspector Garcia asks for them.

Maybe Constable Dad didn't ask the right way.

Tuesday

10.00 AM

Still waiting.

3.00 PM

Still waiting.

6.00 PM

Olive and I watch Episode 21 of *Amelia X, Girl Detective*. Three-quarters of the way through the episode, Amelia and Jock are waiting too. And they are growing impatient.

'This is taking too long,' says Amelia, 'and we're not getting any closer to the villain,

Jock. I think it's time we set the cat among the pigeons.'

I watch the next bit carefully, waiting for the cat. But it does not appear.

'WHERE IS THE CAT?' I ask Olive.

'What cat?'

'THE ONE WHO IS GOING TO BE SET AMONG THE PIGEONS. WHERE IS IT?'

She laughs. 'It's not a real cat, Clara. It's just another way of saying you're going to stir up trouble. Amelia sent an anonymous letter to Colonel Brawn, warning him that his crooked scheme had been discovered. She was hoping he'd get worried and make the mistake that would bring him down at last. And it worked.'

That is interesting.

That is *very* interesting.

8.30 PM

Olive is in the bathroom cleaning her teeth

when her phone buzzes. Aha! It is not a bee. It is not a wasp. It is Jubilee Crystal Simpson being nasty again.

'yor dad is an idiot and u r worse everywun hates u'

It is time to set the cat among the chooks.

(Yes, I know that Amelia X said, 'set the cat among the pigeons'. But what's the point of that? Pigeons would be *scared* of the cat. They would fly away, or get eaten. They are almost as useless as ducks. But chooks would fix their eyes on that cat and march towards it. And the cat would find itself in *big* trouble.)

I choose my words carefully. 'JUBILEE CRYSTAL SIMPSON,' I write. 'I KNOW ABOUT THE SHEEP.'

I wait for a reply. There is none.

Wednesday night

Dear Mum, Dad picked me and Digby up from school this afternoon. We weren't expecting him, so I knew straight away that something was wrong. We put our bikes in the boot of the car and scrambled aboard, and all the time my heart was going thumpety thumpety thump, too hard and fast.

Dad still hadn't said much, but his face was grim, and as soon as we were away from the school, he stopped the car.

'Something's happened,' he said, looking straight ahead. 'Something serious. And I need an honest answer from both of you.'

Digby and I glanced at each other. 'Okay,' we said.

'Did either of you tell anyone about the other night?' said Dad. 'About Digby's sheep going missing? About the tyre tracks and the description?'

'No,' I said. 'You told us not to.'

'How about you, Digby?'

'Me neither,' said Digby. 'Olive and I talked about it at recess, but we made sure no one could hear us.'

'What about your mum? Do you think she might've said anything?'

'She told Dad about it when he phoned last night. But then she said he mustn't tell anyone, so I don't reckon she has. Why?'

Dad leaned forward and rested his forehead on the steering wheel. 'I had a phone call this afternoon from my boss in the city. Says he's had a few reports about my health, and he's worried about me. Says I have to take compassionate leave. A month, starting Saturday morning. He's replacing me with some young bloke who's never even lived in a country town.'

As he talked, I could feel my eyes getting wider and wider. 'Your boss can't do that!'

'He can,' said Dad.

'But you've got a description of the truck at last. And the tyre tracks.'

'That's what I told him. But he wouldn't budge. Says I have to go to the coast for a proper break, and take you with me.' He raised his head. 'And that's why I'm asking you both one more time: did you tell anyone? I need to know, even if it was an accident. Even if you just *hinted* at something. Because it looks to me as if someone's pulling strings. Someone who knows that I'm getting close and is trying to get me out of the way.'

We both swore that we hadn't said anything, and Dad believed us. He started the car again and drove us home without another word.

I don't want Dad to go on compassionate leave,

Mum. He's just starting to come right again, and so am I. So as we went down the main street of Little Dismal, I stared out the window at everyone we passed. Wondering who was pulling strings, and how we could find out before Saturday.

Clara was having a dust bath when we got home, so Digby and I sat on the back step in the shade, trying to work out what we could do to help Dad. Except we couldn't think of anything, so after a while we fell silent.

I didn't know if we should tell Clara about the compassionate leave or not. I was pretty sure Dad wouldn't let her come with us, which meant she'd have to go back to Auntie Gina's.

Would the other chooks be nicer to her now? Or would they bully her?

We were still sitting there when she scrambled

out of the little hollow she'd made, shook the dust from her wings and came trotting across to say hello.

Only it turned out that 'hello' wasn't what she wanted to say.

'Hi, Clara,' said Digby.

She ignored him, and started searching my pockets for my phone, so I put it down in front of her. She bent her head and started tapping away at the keyboard.

'HAS MASTER CRIMINAL JUBILEE CRYSTAL SIMPSON MADE THE MISTAKE THAT WILL BRING HER DOWN AT LAST?'

Digby snorted. 'Jubilee's a master criminal? I wish.'

'Shut up, Digby,' I said. 'Clara, what are you talking about? Why would Jubilee make a mistake?'

'BECAUSE I SENT HER A MESSAGE.'

'When?' I squeaked.

'LAST NIGHT.'

All I could think of was Dad's grim face when he picked us up from school. 'What was the message?'

'I KNOW ABOUT THE SHEEP.'

I groaned. 'But Clara, Dad told us not to say anything. To anyone!'

'I WAS SETTING THE CAT AMONG THE CHOOKS.'

'*What?*' said Digby.

'AMELIA X YESTERDAY'S EPISODE.'

Digby stared at Clara. 'You mean the anonymous letter to Colonel Brawn?'

Clara's little head bobbed up and down. 'YES AND THEN HE MADE THE MISTAKE THAT WOULD BRING HIM DOWN AT LAST.'

I could hardly speak. 'You – you did it because of Amelia X?'

'AND BECAUSE CONSTABLE DAD WAS TAKING TOO LONG TO SOLVE THE CRIME. AMELIA X NEVER TAKES LONGER THAN ONE HOUR.'

Digby and I looked at each other. 'Clara—'

I began. Then I stopped. And started again. 'Clara, you *do* know that—'

I stopped again.

'You have to tell her,' said Digby.

'I know.'

Clara peered up at us, bright-eyed and keen. 'TELL ME WHAT?'

I picked her up and sat her on my lap, with the phone beside her. 'You're a very clever chook,' I said. 'Much cleverer than a lot of humans. But—'

She wriggled. 'BUT WHAT?'

'But you *do* know that Amelia X isn't real. Don't you?'

'OF COURSE SHE IS REAL. I WATCH HER ONCE A WEEK.'

'It's just a TV show,' I said.

'A story,' said Digby.

'A *made-up* story,' I added. 'With actors. There's no such person as Amelia X. That's why she never takes longer than an hour to solve her crimes. Because that's how long the TV episode is.'

'AMELIA X IS NOT REAL?'

'I'm sorry, Clara, I thought you knew.'

Two years ago, one of the school chooks got a bad case of the staggers. For a whole day she couldn't walk straight, but bumbled in circles, bumping into the other chooks with her beak agape.

That's what Clara looked like.

She wobbled off my lap onto the step, and then onto the ground. 'Clara, wait,' I said. But it was clear that she didn't want to talk. She stumbled around the corner of the house and out of sight. And all Digby and I could do was sit there and watch her go.

Love, Olive

Wednesday night

7.00 PM

If *Amelia X, Girl Detective* is a made-up story, does that mean *Death in the City* is also made up? Is Inspector Garcia just an actor?

Have I built my life and my hopes on a falsehood?

8.00 PM

'Clara! Clara, where are you?'

'Clara? Won't you come out, wherever you are? Dad cooked spaghetti.'

Olive and Digby are calling me, but I will not answer, not even for spaghetti.

I thought I was clever. I thought I could be a proper detective.

But I was wrong.

I am a fool.

8.30 PM

'There you are. Digby, she's under Dad's bed. Come out, Clara. Please come out.'

I tuck my head under my wing so Olive can't see me. I shall stay here for the rest of my life. I shall not eat. I shall not drink. Hopefully, everyone will soon forget about me.

Olive wriggles under the bed and lies down next to me. I keep my head under my wing.

'I brought you some spaghetti,' she says. 'It's got meatballs. They're falling apart and look fairly weird, but they taste nice.'

I can smell them. They mean nothing to me.

Olive lies beside me for a while, saying nothing. Then she whispers, 'Dad used to cook all the time. He said it relaxed him after a day at work. Only then—'

She takes a deep breath. 'Then Mum died and he stopped cooking. That's when we started living on baked beans. I didn't mind at first, because I couldn't taste anything. And then everything started going wrong at school, and the baked beans were just another part of it.'

Her hand touches my back. She starts stroking me.

'And then you came,' she whispers. 'You were the first good thing that had happened for ages. You were funny. You were smart. You were my friend. That's when things started to change. And now Dad's cooking again. I don't mean that everything's all right, because it's not. And maybe it never will be, without – without Mum. But it's *better*, Clara, and that's all because of you.'

I suppose it wouldn't hurt if I just looked at the spaghetti, to see if Olive is right about the meatballs.

I lower my wing a little, so that one eye is uncovered. The meatballs are falling apart. They look a bit like dead maggots, which I have always liked.

But I will not be tempted.

'I just wanted to tell you that, because it's important,' says Olive. 'But there's something else. Digby and I think you might be onto something. You know, with Jubilee Crystal Simpson.'

I jerk my head out from under my wing and stare at her.

'Because *I* didn't tell anyone about Digby's sheep being stolen and neither did he. He phoned his mum to check, and she hasn't said a word. And Dad wouldn't have let it slip. So you're the only one. And it might just be a coincidence, Dad getting orders the *very next day* to go on compassionate leave. But it might not. We have to tell him, Clara. Which means you have to come out from under the bed, because he won't believe us unless you're there.'

I peer at the meatballs. Maybe I will eat a little bit.

Still Wednesday night

Dear Mum, you know how Dad sometimes digs his heels in and goes really stubborn? Tonight was one of those times.

I suppose I can't really blame him. It must've been fairly weird to have us march up to him and say, 'Dad, Clara's the one who gave it away.'

He was sitting at the kitchen table, frowning at the screen of his laptop. 'Olive,' he said, 'I haven't got time for games. Just go and talk to Digby, okay? Do a – a jigsaw or something. Or maybe you should start packing.'

'It's not a game, Dad. Clara messaged Jubilee Simpson last night. And I think—'

'We think the two things might be connected,' said Digby. 'We think Clara's message might have set off your phone call. We think you should look more closely at Mr Simpson.'

'I *am* looking at Simpson,' said Dad, without taking his eyes from the screen. 'As well as half a dozen others.'

'Yes, but we think you should *focus* on him,' I said. 'Remember how he promised those CCTV cameras, and set up the roster? So everyone thought he was a really good bloke? But the cameras still haven't turned up, and you said yourself that the roster caused more trouble than it was worth. And now this message of Clara's has—'

Dad interrupted me. 'Okay, you've had your fun. But I mean it about the packing. If I can't figure this out by Friday, I really will have to take leave. And you'll have to come with me.'

He wasn't listening, not properly. So I put Clara on the kitchen table, right next to his laptop.

She inspected the keyboard, then began to

peck at it. But before she could finish a single word, Dad grabbed hold of her and stood up, saying, 'That's enough. Out!'

He thrust Clara into my hands and pushed me and Digby towards the door.

'But Dad—' I said.

'*Enough*, Olive. Go and do something useful.' And he shut the door in our faces.

So we went to my room and had a council of war.

Except first Clara had to finish off the meatballs and groom her feathers. Then she needed to check a few facts.

'IS INSPECTOR GARCIA REAL?'

I shook my head. 'Sorry.'

'SO I WILL NEVER MEET HER AND EXCHANGE STORIES ABOUT OUR MOST PUZZLING CASES?'

'Nope,' said Digby.

'AND CRIMES CANNOT BE SOLVED IN AN HOUR?'

'Definitely not,' I said.

She thought for a moment, then wrote, 'SO WHAT DO WE DO NOW?'

'We've only got until Friday,' said Digby. 'It's not long.'

'We need to find more evidence against the Simpsons,' I said. 'Maybe we could bug their phones.'

'INSTALL HIDDEN CAMERAS IN THEIR HOUSE.'

'Kidnap Jubilee and not give her back until her father confesses,' said Digby.

I pulled a face. 'I'm not going anywhere near her, not if I can help it.'

'She's not so bad at home,' said Digby. 'I've been there a couple of times, and her dad's a bit strange – even jollier than usual, you know? Making jokes and stuff, and whacking you on the back as if you're his best friend. But he hardly takes any notice of Jubilee.'

'You're not making excuses for her, are you?' I asked him.

'No. Well, maybe. A bit.'

'I hate her,' I said. 'I hate her so much I don't even want to kidnap her.'

'Fair enough,' said Digby. 'She's been nasty to you.'

'More than nasty.'

Digby lay back on the bed with his hands behind his head. 'So what are we going to do? Seriously, what *can* we do?'

Clara nudged the phone into a better position and wrote, 'I WILL GO UNDERCOVER.'

We both stared at her.

'What do you mean?' said Digby.

'I WILL PRETEND TO BE ONE OF THEIR CHOOKS.'

'We don't even know if they've got chooks,' I said.

'They have,' said Digby. 'I think they came with the pub, because the Simpsons don't know much about looking after them. But, Clara, you can't go undercover. If they really are the thieves, it's too dangerous.'

'WHO WOULD SUSPECT A CHOOK?'

'Well, no one,' said Digby. 'But still.'

'I WILL TAKE YOUR PHONE DIGBY IT IS SMALLER THAN OLIVE'S. I WILL NEED A BAG TO CARRY IT AROUND MY NECK.'

'You really mean it?' I asked. 'You really want to do this?'

'WE MUST HELP CONSTABLE DAD.'

'Yes, but—'

'WE MUST SOLVE THE CRIME.'

'Yes, but—'

'WE MUST BRING JUBILEE CRYSTAL SIMPSON MASTER CRIMINAL TO JUSTICE.'

Thursday

5.30 AM

Digby is sleeping in the spare bedroom. Olive wakes him up so he can join us for First Squawk.

He does quite well for a beginner.

5.45 AM

We all practise semaphore. I am reminded of Inspector Garcia's last session at the shooting range with her colleagues, just before she went undercover to break up a gang of drug smugglers (Episode 14).

She made jokes. She gave her watch to

Sergeant Jessica Ng, to keep for her until she came back. She reminded her colleagues that justice must prevail.

(I know she is not real, but she is still my hero.)

I do not have a watch, so I will give my egg to Olive for her breakfast. I will remind her and Digby that justice must prevail.

I will try to make a joke, though I am not sure how.

7.30 AM

Olive has made a little bag to hold Digby's phone. She tells me his passcode, then shows me how to take photos and films. She shows me how to send messages. She warns me to watch out for the battery, and not to use the phone unless I have to.

She hugs me.

I peck her ear gently, and check her hair for mites.

8.00 AM

Digby carries me into town on his handlebars. When we are a few doors away from the pub he stops and whispers, 'Good luck, Clara.'

I hop down and scuttle behind a planter box. There are cars parked up and down the street, and people talking on the footpath. I wait until no one is looking in my direction, then I run into the gap between two shops.

My heart is beating fast. From here on, I am on my own.

A man walks towards me, so I scratch at the dirt and hope he doesn't notice the bag around my neck. He passes without a word.

As soon as the coast is clear, I set off for the yard at the back of the pub. I get there just as Jubilee Crystal Simpson rides away on her bike.

What's the point of going undercover in a master criminal's headquarters if the master criminal is not there? I almost turn around and head for the school. But then I change my mind. Perhaps this is for the best. Perhaps I can dig up some evidence while she's gone.

8.45 AM

The good news is, the Simpsons don't have a rooster. The bad news is, they have a very bossy chief hen.

As soon as I walk into the yard, she bustles up with a fierce expression, flapping her wings and saying, *'Who are you? What are you doing in my yard? Explain yourself.'*

I lift my wing to reveal my police badge – only to realise that I took it off to try out the phone bag, and never put it on again.

I can't be a police officer without a badge. Where's my authority? Who will listen to me?

But I can't turn back, either.

'*Sorry to bother you, ma'am,*' I say, '*but I believe there's a gang of rats holed up in the pub. According to my sources, they're notorious egg stealers.*'

That gets her attention. '*Egg-stealing rats? Near MY yard?*'

'*GIANT egg-stealing rats,*' I tell her.

If this hen was a rooster, she'd be racing around the yard shouting a warning. Instead, she arches her neck and says, '*How can we help?*'

'*I don't want them to know I'm onto them,*' I say. '*So it's best if you and your sisters just go about your business as usual. Pretend I'm one of the flock. I'll let you know if I need anything more.*'

She hurries off to warn her sisters. They cluck and fuss, and stare at me, but then they go back to their scratching.

I hide Digby's phone under an old

wheelbarrow, then wander towards the back door, scratching at the dirt and catching the occasional grasshopper as I go.

The back door opens onto a small room. There are coats hanging on hooks, and two sets of boots lined up beside another door, which is also open. I cluck quietly to myself, and creep past the boots and into the kitchen.

There are no humans around. There is, however, a large grey tomcat asleep under the kitchen table.

I creep up to him and squawk loudly in his ear. He wakes up with a yowl of fright. I peck his furry tail, and say, 'Scram,' and he races out the back door with his fur standing on end and his ears flattened against his head.

Enemy number one dealt with.

Now that the coast is clear, I trot back outside for the phone. I set it up in a dark corner of the kitchen, ready for filming. Then I hide behind the fridge.

10.00 AM

No one comes into the kitchen for some time. I do Nap.

11.00 AM

Still no one, so I pop outside for a quick dust bath and a chat with the bossy hen, whose name is Delilah. She doesn't know anything much about the Simpsons, except that they often forget to collect the eggs.

12.00 PM

I go back inside, hop up onto the edge of the

rubbish bin and investigate the leftovers. I'm just getting stuck into half a loaf of bread when I hear footsteps.

I leave the bread where it is and dive back into hiding, just as Mr Simpson comes into the kitchen, talking on his phone.

I'm about to tap out the passcode and press record on Digby's phone when I remember what Olive said about the battery. I'd better wait until someone does something illegal.

'Well, maybe it's for the best, Noelene,' says Mr Simpson in his Merrycan accent. 'Some people just don't look after themselves well enough, you know what I mean? He's a great cop, but I don't think he took the time to grieve.'

He's talking about Constable Dad! Quickly I press the record button.

'What's that, Noelene?' says Mr Simpson. 'Well, of course we'll miss him! He's one of this little town's greatest assets. But he'll be back, better than ever. And in the meantime I'm sure they'll send us a good replacement. Maybe we should put our heads together sometime over the weekend and figure out a rousing welcome for the new feller. Saturday night suit you? Here, eight o'clock? Sure, invite whoever you like. That's the way, Noelene. I knew I could count on you. Take care now.'

2.00 PM

Undercover work is supposed to be exciting (*Death in the City*, Episode 6). But it's not. There are no drug raids. No murders. No bodies buried in the backyard. (If there were, Delilah would have dug them up by now. For the maggots.)

Jubilee Crystal Simpson has *no idea* how to be a good master criminal.

3.30 PM

Jubilee Crystal Simpson is home from school. Now at last I should see something interesting.

She sits at the kitchen table. She stares at her phone, which is smaller than Digby's.

This is not interesting.

5.00 PM

Still not interesting. I pop outside for a quick Earwig O'Clock.

Delilah sidles up to me and says, out of the

corner of her beak, *'Any news on the giant rats?'*

'I'm closing in on them,' I tell her. *'But it's a dangerous business, and I can't rush things.'*

'Let us know if you need backup,' she says.

Delilah is a chook after my own heart. I wonder if she watches *Death in the City*.

Thursday night

Dear Mum, waiting is the hardest thing. Digby went home for a little while after school, but then he came back here. We're not doing anything much, just sitting around trying not to look at my phone.

Trying not to wait for a message from Clara.

Dad's still at work. He's been there all day, except for an hour at dinnertime. We quizzed him about the Simpsons and he admitted that he's been looking at them more closely. And he found out something about the roster of people who've been keeping an eye on the roads.

'The night your sheep were taken,' he said to Digby, through a mouthful of sausage, 'Jake

Bester was supposed to be watching Wattle Hut Road. But round about one AM he got a text to say there'd been a mix-up and he was meant to be on Yabby Creek Road. He didn't know who the text was from, but the whole roster thing has been a bit chaotic from the sound of it, so he just assumed it was someone who knew what they were doing. He went off to the other road and didn't think any more of it.'

Dad speared another sausage. I wanted to tell him to eat more slowly because he'd get hiccups, but I was afraid he'd stop talking, so I didn't.

'And because no one knows that was the night the thieves struck,' he said, 'no one asked any questions.'

'Did you tell him?' asked Digby.

Dad grinned. Not a nice grin. A *fierce* grin. 'Nope. Not a word.'

He swallowed the last bit of sausage, looked at his watch and stood up. 'I'd better get back to work.'

And then he was gone, leaving Digby and me to wait and worry. Digby's staying over again tonight, which is just as well, because I couldn't bear it here by myself.

I just hope Clara's okay. What if we don't hear from her? What will we do then?

Love, Olive

Friday

5.30 AM

First Squawk. The Simpsons are not awake yet, so I join in with Delilah and her flock. It is not the same as doing First Squawk with Olive, but it is better than being alone.

6.30 AM

Worm Hunt. The Simpsons are still not awake. I wonder if there is a rooster somewhere nearby who could crow under their bedroom windows. I need them up and talking, and giving themselves away. Or murdering someone so I can film them.

(As long as it's not Delilah they murder. She is a chook of taste and intelligence.)

7.00 AM

Egg O'Clock. I am not, repeat *not* leaving my beautiful egg where Jubilee Crystal Simpson might find it. Delilah tells me that the neighbours are nice and sometimes throw cooked rice over the fence. So I go next door and lay my egg under their letterbox.

8.00 AM

The Simpsons are awake at last! I wait until the back door is open and they are not looking, and I creep into the kitchen. The cat is asleep under the table again, so I peck its nose. Then I stare at it until it runs away.

Even Delilah is impressed by my stare.

9.30 AM

Jubilee has gone to school and Mr Simpson

has gone out. It is a long, slow morning. The Simpsons are not very good at being criminals. Nonetheless, I stay in my hiding spot behind the rubbish bin, with Digby's phone set at just the right angle to catch them if they murder someone.

1.00 PM

Still no bodies, except for the dead mouse under the fridge. I check that it hasn't been poisoned, then eat it.

3.30 PM

Jubilee comes home from school. She sits at the table and stares at her phone.

Is that suspicious? Probably not.

I'm beginning to wonder if I've made a mistake. Maybe I am watching the wrong master criminal.

4.00 PM

Mr Simpson's phone buzzes as he walks into the kitchen. He scowls, puts it to his ear and snaps, 'What is it? I told you not to call me.'

His voice sounds different. The Merrycan accent has gone, and so has the friendliness.

I tap out the passcode and start recording.

'Yes, Hennessey's leaving tomorrow,' says Mr Simpson. 'And I have it on good authority that his replacement is useless ... What? ... No, it was the only truck I could get at such short notice ... Good, we'll move them tomorrow night ... Now turn your phone off and don't call me again.' He shoves his phone back in his pocket.

I *was* watching the wrong person. The master criminal isn't Jubilee. It's her father!

I'm so excited that I accidentally hit the stop button with my claw, and Digby's phone makes a little beeping sound.

Mr Simpson spins around. 'What was that?'

'It sounded like a phone,' says Jubilee.

My feathers stand on end. She hasn't got a Merrycan accent either! And now Mr Simpson is stalking across the kitchen, like Rufus when he spies a rat. His eyes are hard. His neck is stiff. He's coming straight towards me.

There's no time to wriggle the phone into its bag, and if I try to drag it, the noise will give me away. So I leave it where it is and dive behind the fridge with my head down.

Mr Simpson finds the phone. 'What the— It's been recording me!'

His anger is like the anger of a dozen roosters. He scans the kitchen, and I stand so still that an ant marches across my foot, thinking I'm just a bump in the ground. (I'm not.)

What would Inspector Garcia do in this situation? What would Amelia X do? I have no idea. I don't remember a single episode where either of them crouched trembling behind a fridge.

'Whose phone is it?' asks Jubilee.

'Digby someone. Do you know him?'

'Show me. That's Digby Carella, he's in my class. He's Olive Hennessey's cousin.'

Mr Simpson snarls through his teeth. 'They're onto us. We're going to have to cut things short.'

'Does that mean we can leave this dump?' asks Jubilee.

Her father is drumming his fingers on the table. 'Shut up and let me think. I knew Hennessey was close, but I didn't think he was this close. We'd better move that last lot of sheep tonight, just in case. And then we'll disappear. Jubilee, go and pack.'

He takes his own phone out of his pocket and puts it to his ear. 'Derek? ... Derek, turn on your phone ... No, I don't want to leave a message. Turn on your phone!'

He snaps at Jubilee, his voice as hard and sharp as a dozen beaks. 'I said, go and pack!'

She runs out of the kitchen, while I crouch

even lower, trying to make myself as small as possible. Mr Simpson's going to move the sheep. He's going to get away, and I can't stop him. Without Digby's phone, I can't even tell Olive what's happening.

'Derek? Derek! Turn your phone on, blast you!'

Another person talking about explosions. I hope Mr Simpson doesn't have a bomb. He's terrifying enough without one.

4.30 PM

Mr Simpson's Merrycan accent is back, and so is his friendliness. 'Shirley?' he says into his phone. 'It's Ernie Simpson here. Sorry for the short notice, but can you work the bar tonight? I've had some bad news about my mom … Pneumonia … Yes, it's a worry being so far away … That's a kind thought, Shirley … Just leave the key in the usual place … You can't beat a small town for honesty, can you … Thanks, Shirley.'

I have to tell Olive what's happening, but Mr Simpson is prowling around the kitchen, phoning Derek over and over again. If I try to sneak away, he'll see me. If I run round in circles squawking with fright (which is what I really want to do), he'll see me. If I do anything at all other than crouch behind the fridge, he'll see me.

5.30 PM

At last Mr Simpson summons Jubilee and says, 'I'm not waiting any longer. We'll catch up with Derek on the way. Go and get your suitcase.'

Jubilee hurries out of the room again, and her father follows her. As soon as he's gone, I dash out the back door and run round in circles squawking, to relieve some of my terror. Then I stop. I must do something. But what? Mr Simpson is so big and fierce, and I am so small.

Delilah has seen my distress, and comes over to ask what's wrong.

'Everything,' I tell her. 'The rats are worse than I thought, and now they are escaping.'

'That's good,' she says. 'We'll be rid of them. They'll steal someone else's eggs instead of ours.'

I want to agree with her. I want to cower behind the woodshed until Mr Simpson is gone, and I am safe again. But I am supposed to be a detective. I am supposed to be on the side of truth and justice.

'They might come back,' I say. 'It would be better if we could stop them altogether.'

Before I can say more, the back door slams shut, and Mr Simpson and Jubilee hurry across the yard towards their yellow car, carrying suitcases and coats.

'Where are the rats?' asks Delilah.

In Episode 8 of Death in the City, Inspector Garcia had a moment of sheer desperation. Now I know how she felt.

I mean, I know how she *would* have felt. If she was real.

'The rats are in the suitcases,' I say quickly. *'I have to get into that car without being seen. Wait until the humans open the car doors, then make a fuss. A big one!'*

Without waiting to see if she agrees, I edge towards the car. The Simpsons don't even look at me – after all, I am only a chook.

They put their suitcases in the boot. Mr Simpson opens the driver's door. Jubilee opens the door behind him and tosses in a coat …

Delilah lets out an earsplitting squawk. *'Mouse! I've got a mouse!'* And she begins to run around the car.

Every chook in the yard races after her. *'Mine!'* they shout. *'Give it to me!'* *'Mine mine mine!'*

'What the—' says Mr Simpson, backing up against the car.

Jubilee hides behind her father. While their

attention is elsewhere, I hop up onto the back seat and squirm under Jubilee's coat.

Delilah and her sisters run around the car three more times, then Delilah squawks, *'Oh no, it got away.'* And the noise and the shouting stops as suddenly as it began.

Mr Simpson climbs into the driver's seat, snarling, 'I hate chooks. Next one I see, I'm going to wring its neck.'

Jubilee gets in the back, and her father talks to the car. 'Come on, you stupid thing,' he growls. 'Start, or you'll go to the wreckers.'

He is not at all polite, but the car starts anyway. Jubilee watches the back of her father's head for a moment or two, then takes out her phone and puts white plugs into her ears.

My heart is beating so fast I can hardly think. I huddle down and don't make a sound as we roll out of the yard and away from any chance of safety.

Friday after school

Dear Mum, I've packed. So has Dad. He worked at the station all last night and most of today, and he still can't find enough evidence to charge anyone.

His fierce grin is gone. I want to hug him, but then I'd cry, which would probably make him feel even worse.

Maybe Clara will phone. But I don't think she will, and neither does Digby.

Love, Olive

Friday

5.45 PM

The road is bumpy, and I have to hang on to the coat with my beak to make sure it doesn't slide off me. But if I'm very careful, I can look out between the buttons and see Jubilee, who is listening to something that goes *thunka thunka thunka*.

'I feel sick,' she says.

'If you'd stop listening to that rubbish,' says Mr Simpson, 'you'd be fine.'

More bumps. We turn a corner and the car stops. Jubilee opens her door. Mr Simpson says, 'Don't get out. We won't be here long.'

'But—'

'*Don't* get out.'

Jubilee taps her phone, and the *thunka thunka thunka* gets louder.

'Turn it off,' says Mr Simpson.

She ignores him.

'Turn it off or I'll leave you here in the middle of nowhere and you can make your own way back to Melbourne.'

'You wouldn't.'

'Try me,' growls Mr Simpson.

With a scowl, Jubilee rips the plugs out of her ears and throws her phone on top of the coat.

On top of *me*.

Mr Simpson climbs out of the car, bellowing, 'Derek? Derek, where are you?'

If I could get hold of Jubilee's phone, I could send an urgent message to Olive. But if I move, Jubilee will see me and tell her father, and he'll wring my neck.

I crouch lower, wishing Olive was here. Or Constable Dad. (Though neither of them would fit under this coat.) They'd know what to do.

Footsteps crunch on the gravel as Mr Simpson walks back to the car with another man. 'We can't take the risk,' says Mr Simpson. 'Move them as soon it gets dark, to the usual place.'

He opens his car door to get in – and I make my move. Before Jubilee can shut *her* door, I wriggle out from underneath the coat, snatch up her phone, and jump out of the car.

Behind me, Jubilee screams, 'A chook's got my phone!' And she leaps out of the car too.

I'm already halfway across the yard, frantically clutching the phone in my beak and looking for a hiding place. There's a farmhouse on one side of me and a couple of old car bodies on the other. I run towards the cars, as fast as I can.

'My phone!' wails Jubilee, running after me.

'Leave it,' shouts Mr Simpson.

'No,' cries Jubilee. 'Help me get it back or I won't go.'

'You'll go where I tell you,' shouts Mr Simpson. But when I take a quick look behind

me, he and Derek are coming to help her.

Coming to catch me.

Coming to wring my neck.

I dodge around the car bodies, and dash towards an open-fronted shed on the other side of the yard. Once I'm inside, I dive under a tractor, run past some rotting hay bales and a stack of tyres, and huddle into a corner behind a pile of rusty tools, where they won't see me. Somewhere in the distance, sheep are bleating.

Jubilee gets down on her hands and knees to peer under the tractor. Mr Simpson grabs a stick and pokes viciously at the hay. Derek kicks the tyres.

If Mr Simpson is like a dozen roosters, Derek is a dozen rats. His face is narrow and mean, and there's something about him that makes me shrink even further into the corner.

'Listen, Ernie,' he says, 'I don't like this new truck. It's too open. Anyone drives up behind me, they'll see the sheep.'

'I told you, it was the only one I could get at such short notice,' says Mr Simpson. 'We can't use the old one, not if they're onto us. Hang a tarpaulin over the back and sides if you're worried.'

They've stopped searching, and are leaning against the hay bales. I'm in the corner, trying to send an urgent message to Olive. Jubilee's phone doesn't have a passcode, which should make it easy. But it's completely different from Olive's and Digby's phones, and I can't find the messages.

The only thing I recognise is the camera.

I turn it on, creep forward and prop the phone in the narrow gap between a spade and a garden fork.

'If I get caught—' says Derek.

'You won't get caught. And if you do, I'll get you the best lawyers in the country – as long as you keep your mouth shut.'

'I'd still rather wait a couple of days,' says Derek, 'until Hennessey's gone.'

'If he's got his eye on me,' says Mr Simpson, 'he might know about you. And it won't be hard to find this place once he starts looking. Get rid of the sheep tonight, and then we all disappear. No more Ernie Simpson. No more Derek Black. No more sheep.' He laughs, hard and nasty. 'Not here, anyway.'

'What are you laughing about?' cries Jubilee, from the other side of the shed. 'Come and help me look for my phone!'

Mr Simpson and Derek roll their eyes at each other and go to help her. I turn off the camera. It has evidence inside it now, proper evidence that Constable Dad will want to see. I need to get it to him.

I slide the phone into the bag around my

neck, then I creep out of the shed and make a dash for the car.

The doors are still open, so I hop up onto the driver's seat and quickly apologise for not introducing myself earlier. *'I was in a bit of a rush,'* I say to the car. *'And I still am. Could you take me to the police station, please, before the criminals come back? I have important evidence for Constable Dad.'*

The car doesn't respond. I try again. *'Don't*

let me down, old girl,' I squawk. 'Start nicely, now. That's it, that's the way. Good girl!'

Still nothing. So I try Mr Simpson's method. 'Come on, you stupid thing. Start, or you'll go to the wreckers!'

The car just sits there, taking no notice of me. I can't afford to waste any more time on such a rude, unhelpful creature – Mr Simpson and Derek will be back soon and they mustn't catch me.

But just as I'm about to hop down, I see a shiny silver badge hanging next to the steering wheel on a silver ring.

Why has this car got a badge? Badges are for *helpful* people, like the roosters. And me.

I grab the ring in my beak and pull it out of the hole it's stuck in. There's a little silver stick attached to it, which makes it even nicer.

'You don't deserve such a fine

thing,' I tell the car. And when I hop down, I take the badge, the ring and the silver stick with me.

I hurry across the yard to the corner of the house, and settle into a spot where I can watch both the shed and the car without being seen. Then I put the silver badge down carefully beside me, take the phone out of its bag and try once again to find the messages.

But I've run out of time. Mr Simpson is marching back to the car, brushing cobwebs and dust from his clothes. 'We have to go,' he says.

'What about my *phone*?' wails Jubilee.

'Is there anything incriminating on it?'

'No.'

'And did you put a passcode on it when I told you to?'

'Um – yes,' mumbles Jubilee.

'Then it doesn't matter if you lose it. I'll get you another one in Melbourne.'

Jubilee tries to argue, but her father ignores her. He says a few final words to Derek, then he and Jubilee climb into the car and slam their doors.

I peck frantically at the phone. How can I get a message to Olive? The car's about to leave, and—

But it's *not* leaving. Instead, the driver's door flies open and Mr Simpson climbs out, checking his pockets. 'Derek, have you seen my car keys?'

6.30 PM

Mr Simpson is swearing and searching for his keys. (I don't know what keys are, but I'm glad he lost them.) Jubilee is back in the shed, looking for her phone. Derek leans against one of the car bodies with his eyes shut.

I'm trying to work out how to send a message to Olive.

7.00 PM

Mr Simpson is still searching for his keys. He's storming around the yard now, red-faced and swollen with anger. If he had feathers, they'd be bristling.

I'm still trying to work out how to send a message, but Mr Simpson's anger makes it hard to think. So does the trembling in my legs and wings.

7.30 PM

After a lot of shouting, Derek and the Simpsons have gone inside the house. My legs have stopped trembling and I've found the messages at last. But I don't know Olive's phone number.

7.45 PM

Mr Simpson and Derek come out of the house. Mr Simpson is still angry, but now it's a cold, hard fury that's even got Derek treading carefully. They start wiping down the car with a towel, inside and out. They're cleaning away the fingerprints, just like the mob boss in Episode 10 of *Death in the City*.

Except the mob boss was nowhere near as scary as Mr Simpson.

'Get those sheep loaded into the truck,' he snarls over his shoulder to Derek. 'We're leaving as soon it gets dark.'

8.00 PM

I've found the nasty messages that Jubilee sent. And there's Olive's phone number! I send a new message.

'SIMPSONS ESCAPING SHEEP AT DEREKS FARM COME QUICKLY'

I haven't got time for full stops. I hope it makes sense.

8.10 PM

Olive hasn't replied yet.

I can hear a truck now – Derek is on the move. I don't want to go after him. I want to stay where I am, hidden from Mr Simpson's anger.

But Olive still hasn't replied to my message. So I gather up my courage, shove the phone and the silver badge into the bag, poke my head through the loop and run out of the shed.

I follow the sound of the sheep down a rough road to a yard, where a blue truck is backed up to a gate. Derek is waving his arms at the sheep and shouting, 'Hoy! Hoy! Up you go, up the ramp, that's right. No, not that way, stupid.'

I creep as close to him as I dare, and wait until another sheep tries to escape. As Derek turns to grab it, I dash past him, up the ramp and into the far corner of the truck, where I hide behind a forest of woolly legs.

Derek pushes the runaway sheep up the ramp after me, and shuts the back of the truck. He walks around to climb into the driver's seat, and the truck rumbles to life and carries us towards the house.

The top of the truck is open to the sky, but there are canvas flaps nailed to the back and sides, so I can't see out. I stare at the nearest sheep instead, and she stares back at me.

'Pleased to meet you,' I squawk. 'Clara, Chook of Mystery, at your service.'

I don't think she understands me, so I introduce myself to the truck with the same words. It rumbles quietly, which is more than the car did.

We stop at the house, where Jubilee is

complaining again. 'Can we just leave?' she wails. 'I'm sick of this place.'

'Put the luggage in the cabin so it doesn't get dirty,' orders Mr Simpson. 'We'll pick up a rental car as soon as we get to a decent-sized town.'

Jubilee grumbles a bit more, then loads the luggage and climbs up into the truck. A bit later, Mr Simpson joins her, and we set off.

Mr Simpson and Derek are not safe to be around, and neither are the sheep. They have hard hooves, and they don't at all mind treading on the detective who is trying to rescue them.

I squawk softly at them to remind them I'm here. I suggest they lie down, so that they won't fall on top of me every time we go over a bump or around a corner. They take no notice.

Olive has not come. I start unpicking the bottom corner of one of the flaps with my beak, so I can see where we are going.

Friday night

Dear Mum, Digby and I were in the middle of washing up when my phone buzzed. I grabbed it out of my pocket so fast I nearly dropped it in the water.

Except the message came from that anonymous phone, not Digby's, so I didn't open it. I thought it was just Jubilee being nasty again.

But Digby kept asking who it was from, so in the end I told him about all the horrible messages, and he wanted to see them. And when I gave in and opened up the new one to show him, it was from Clara!

At least, *I* thought it was. Digby wasn't so sure.

'Why didn't she use my phone?' he said. 'And who's Derek?'

'Isn't that Mr Talbot's name? Out near the tip?'

'No, said Digby, 'he's Darren.' He grabbed my phone and called his mum. 'Hi Mum ... yes, we're fine. Listen, is there a farmer anywhere near here called Derek? ... no, I didn't think so ... no reason, see ya.'

We looked at each other, the washing up forgotten. 'What if it's Jubilee playing some sort of trick?' said Digby.

'Why would she message me about her and her dad escaping? It has to be Clara,' I said. 'It *sounds* like Clara. I'm going to message her back.'

'where r u?' I wrote.

No answer.

'wheres the farm?'

No answer.

'whos derek?'

No answer.

Now we don't know what to do. Dad's gone

to bed early cos he's so tired, and I don't want to wake him up until we've got something definite.

Come on, Clara. If that was you, we need more. Come on!

Love, Olive

Still Friday

8.40 PM

At last I've unpicked the corner of the flap, and can see out. Not that there's much to see. Fences, mostly, whizzing past. And the moon coming up over the trees.

I feel a strong urge to hop up onto the back of one of the sheep and go to sleep, but instead I check the phone. Olive has replied at last, with a list of questions, which I do my best to answer, though some of them are just plain silly.

'where r u?'

'I'M HERE' (I would have thought that was obvious.)

'wheres the farm?'

'FORGET FARM THEY HAVE SHEEP ON TRUCK COME AND ARREST THEM'

'whos derek?'

'GIANT RAT'

The truck speeds around a corner. Another message comes through from Olive. 'wheres the truck?'

Another silly question. 'IT'S HERE!!!!!'

'wot can u see?'

That one is more sensible, so I peer under the flap, watching for something useful, like a road sign saying in big letters, 'YOU ARE

3 KM NORTH OF LITTLE DISMAL, ON THE YABBY CREEK ROAD.'

But there are no road signs.

There are, however, three big towers, looming up against the night sky. The Boss calls them silos. So that's what I tell Olive.

'3 SILOS ON SIDE OF ROAD'

Seconds later, Olive messages me back. 'hang on clara we r coming'

I hang on.

8.50 PM

We've left the bumpy road behind, and the truck is travelling smoothly. Most of the sheep have fallen asleep on their feet. I'm still crouched by the hole in the flap.

A car passes us.

A little while later, another car passes us.

We pass a truck.

And suddenly it strikes me. How will Olive know which truck I'm in? Did I tell her it was BLUE? I don't think so.

I tap the phone with my claw until it lights up. Only it *doesn't* light up, not very well. And when I peer at it closely, there's a message on the screen.

Please connect your phone to the charger

I hardly have time to read it before the screen goes dark.

I peck that phone as hard as I can. I argue

with it. I call it 'old girl', as if it was a car, and explain how important it is that it wakes up again.

It takes no notice.

Another car passes us. What if that was Olive and Constable Dad? What if they've driven straight past, not realising that the blue truck is the right truck? What if they never find me?

I am going to have to take desperate measures.

I leave the phone next to the hole and flap up onto the back of one of the sleeping sheep. She sways from side to side with the movement of the truck, and I have to dig my claws into her wool so I don't fall off.

But where can I go from here? What I need is a really tall sheep. Or a series of them, so I can climb them like a ladder. Unfortunately, all Digby's sheep are the same size. (If we are ever rescued, I will complain to him about this.)

I crane my neck. There are four wooden bars running across the top of the truck, from one side to the other. One near the back, one near the front, and two in between. That's where I need to be, right up there on those wooden bars.

Amelia X crosses her fingers before she attempts a dangerous feat, and says, 'Wish me luck, Jock.'

I try to cross my wing feathers but can't. So I say, *'Wish me luck, sheep.'* Then I launch myself into the air.

I overheard the Boss say once that she would love to be able to fly. I don't know why she said it – flying isn't easy. I flap my wings as hard as I can, but I don't get anywhere near those wooden bars.

With a squawk, I fall back onto the sheep, who bleats a sleepy protest. I sit there for a few moments, catching my breath and hoping that Mr Simpson, master criminal and angry wringer of necks, didn't hear me.

Then I try again, but this time I don't aim for the wooden bars high above my head. Instead, I aim for the one that runs halfway up across the back of the cabin.

I get there on my second try.

I cling to the bar, panting. There's a window just above me, and if I stand on my toes I can see Derek at the wheel, and the Simpsons perched on top of their luggage like Great-Aunt Isabel sitting on her eggs, only nastier.

I take a quick look, then crouch down again so they don't see me.

From here, it's not nearly as far to the place I need to be. I straighten my feathers, take a deep breath and launch myself upwards.

I'm aiming for the bar that is second from the front. But just as I reach it, the wind seizes me – and carries me straight past the second bar towards the back of the truck.

I try to grab the third bar, but the wind carries me past that one too. I'm about to be blown right off the truck, far from home, in a place where Olive will never find me.

It's such a terrible thought that I flap harder than I have ever flapped in my life. One of my claws touches the fourth and last bar. I grab hold of it just in time – and find myself hanging by one leg over the back of the truck with my wings above my head and all my feathers blown up the wrong way.

I'm sure nothing like this ever happened to Inspector Garcia.

After a mighty struggle, I manage to fasten my other claw onto the bar, and gradually drag myself upright.

The wind is still blowing fiercely through my feathers, and every instinct tells me to turn around and face towards it, so that my feathers will lie smooth and comfortable.

Instead I stand there shivering, and wait for the next car.

Friday night again

Dear Mum, Dad might be tired, but he leaped out of bed when I told him about the message, and pulled his uniform on over his pyjamas. I didn't tell him it was from Clara – I knew he wouldn't believe it. I just said I'd got a message about the truck, and he assumed it was from Matey. (He still thinks Matey is a kid in my class.)

I didn't lie to him, Mum, honest I didn't. I told him that according to *my informant* the truck carrying Digby's sheep had just passed the Potters' place – you know, where those silos are on White Kangaroo Road?

We were about to pile into the police car, when

Dad stopped and looked at Digby and me really hard. 'Are you sure you trust this person?'

'Yes,' I told him. 'I trust them completely.'

Because I do, Mum. Clara might have some weird ideas, but that's just because she's a chook and sees the world a bit differently. She's been right about all the important things, and I should have listened to her earlier than I did.

Dad jumped into the car. I scrambled in next to him, and Digby climbed in the back.

Dad was fierce and determined at the wheel. Digby and I were fierce and determined watching my phone and hoping for another message from Clara.

It didn't take us long to get to the Potters' place. We whizzed past the silos without talking, but we hadn't gone much further when Dad said, 'Keep your eyes open for a white truck. Late-model Isuzu.'

So we watched the road ahead. We didn't know how far behind the truck we were, and Dad was hitting the speed limit all the way. I was feeling sick again, but this time it was from excitement.

There wasn't much traffic on the road. We passed three cars. We passed a van. We passed a blue truck with tarpaulins on its sides and its top shrouded in darkness. But we couldn't find a *white* truck, which was the only one we cared about.

My excited-sick feeling began to turn into worried-sick.

Dad said, 'You're sure about your informant?'

'Yes,' said Digby and I together.

We kept driving. But there was no white truck. No stolen sheep. No Clara.

None of us looked fierce and determined now. The hope was draining out of us, and we were slumped in our seats, rubbing our eyes and yawning.

When we came to the T-junction where White Kangaroo Road joins the Dismal Road, Dad pulled onto the shoulder and sat there, gripping the steering wheel. The yellow lights over the intersection shone on his face.

'Which way?' he asked. 'Left or right?'

'I don't know,' I whispered.

He looked at me and tried to smile. 'No more messages from your informant?'

I shook my head. 'I'm sorry, Dad.'

He sighed. 'Well, at least we gave it a good go.'

'Are we going home?' I asked him.

'I don't know what else we can do,' he said.

We all sighed then.

'They've won,' Digby said sadly. 'The thieves have won.'

Still Friday night

9.30 PM

There's a car behind the truck, but its head-lights don't quite reach me up here. Is it Olive or a complete stranger? Can they even see me? I have no way of knowing. So I put my plan into action and hope for the best.

It's hard to do semaphore in a strong wind. My wings fly in all directions and I wobble dreadfully. I just hope Olive can read my message.

'S-T-O-P T-H-I-S T-R-U-C-K'

I spell it out twice, just in case. Then I wait, teetering on the bar.

The car pulls out from behind the truck and drives away into the distance.

It can't have been Olive.

9.45 PM

I have spelled out my message five times for five lots of headlights. My wings are aching and I am shivering with cold. I can't do this much longer.

I wish I knew where Olive was. Maybe she and Constable Dad have taken the wrong road. Maybe they went to the wrong three silos.

Maybe they turned back, unable to find me.

9.55 PM

Another car. And another.

No one is coming to help me, not now. I'm lost. Perhaps I will be carried away to the city, where there are car chases and diamond thieves. Or perhaps Mr Simpson, master criminal, will catch me and wring my neck.

I should be excited about the diamond thieves, and scared of Mr Simpson. But I'm too tired to care about anything or anyone.

Except Olive.

I thought she was my sidekick, but she's not. She's my friend, and I mustn't let her down.

With my last bit of strength, I raise my wings and spell out the message one more time.

Friday night again

Dear Mum, Dad turned the car around, so we were facing back the way we'd come. He couldn't pull out onto the road straight away, because the blue truck we'd passed earlier was coming towards us.

So we waited.

The blue truck reached the T-junction and turned right.

I blinked. In the yellow light, I thought I saw a small brave figure clinging to the top of the truck.

'Clara!' I shrieked. 'It's Clara!'

Dad had been easing the car out onto the road, to go back home. But now he jammed on his brakes. 'What?'

'Follow that blue truck, Dad,' I said. 'Follow that truck!'

He is the best dad in the whole world. He didn't ask questions, he just spun the wheel so that we skidded out into the road, and turned right.

It didn't take us long to catch up with the blue truck. But as we came up behind it, the same thing happened as last time. Dad had his headlights on low beam so as not to shine in the driver's rear-vision mirror, which meant we *couldn't see the top of the truck*.

I chewed my fingernails. Digby reached over from the back seat and grabbed my hand, and I chewed *his* fingernails. 'Dad,' I said, 'could you put your headlights on high beam? Just for a moment?'

He looked at me. 'Please?' I said.

He flicked the high-beam switch. The top of the truck lit up. And there, teetering on top of it with her wings flapping madly, was Clara.

Dad stared and stared. 'It really is …'

'Yes!' I cried. 'It's her!'

'But what's she *doing*?'

'Um,' I said. 'Could it be semaphore?'

Dad shook his head. 'You're trying to tell me that Clara is doing – semaphore?'

'She's really good at it,' I said. 'She taught me.'

'And me,' said Digby.

'Of course she did,' said Dad, in a strained voice. 'So – what's she saying? In semaphore.'

I spelled out the letters one by one. 'S-T-A-B T-H-O-S T-R-I-C-K. What's that supposed to mean? Stab thos trick? It doesn't make sense.'

Digby bounced in his seat. 'She's getting it wrong because of the wind. She means *stop this truck!*'

He was right. I turned back to Dad. 'You have to stop the truck, Dad. Clara wouldn't say it unless it was important.'

'You want me to stop the truck? On the word of a – a chook?'

'*Yes!*' Digby and I said together.

Dad swallowed. 'And I'm going to do it. I must be mad.'

'You're not a duck, Dad,' I said.

'*What?*'

'Nothing. Just stop the truck.'

That fierce expression came back to his face. He flicked his headlights to low beam. He pulled out from behind the truck. He turned on the siren.

Digby and I were both bouncing now. We stared at the truck as we passed it, but couldn't see who was driving. Was Mr Simpson there? Was Jubilee? Was I going to get to see Dad arrest her?

Dad pulled in front of the truck with the siren

still going, and began to slow down, so the truck had to slow too. We stopped by the side of the road and Dad put on his hat and picked up his torch.

'If you come with me, you've got to keep your mouths shut,' he said. 'Not a word out of either of you.' And we all piled out of the car.

Dad walked back to the truck, where the driver had wound down the window. He wore a baseball cap that shadowed his face, and a checked shirt.

He had passengers, though I couldn't quite see who they were. They must've been sitting on something, because their heads nearly touched the roof.

'I wasn't breaking the speed limit, was I, mate?' asked the driver. He sounded friendly, as if this was just an ordinary stop, and he had nothing at all to worry about.

Dad said, in his best policeman manner, 'Could I see your driver's licence, sir?'

The man handed over his licence. Dad switched on his torch and studied it. 'Derek Black. Is that you, sir?'

'Yeah, that's me,' said the man. He added, 'Taillights should be okay. I checked them yesterday.'

'Your taillights are in good order,' said Dad.

He shone his torch into the cabin. And there, blinking in the light, were Mr Simpson and Jubilee!

'G'day, Ernie,' said Dad. 'G'day, Jubilee. What are you doing here?'

Mr Simpson blinked again. Then he smiled widely and said, 'Dave Hennessey, is that you? Well, I'll be – this is great. This is just great.'

He threw open the passenger door, saying, 'Hop down, Jubilee. Constable Hennessey's here to help us.'

The two of them scrambled out of the truck, and Mr Simpson strode around to shake hands with Dad. 'You wouldn't believe the day we've had,' he said. 'What with my mom falling sick and trying to get last-minute plane tickets.' He shook his head. 'But I thought we were on our way at last, and so we were, until our car broke down.'

He waved a hand at the truck driver. 'We would have been lost if it wasn't for this kind gent who picked us up back down the road a bit. Now he's driving us to the next town, so we can hire a car to take us to the airport.'

He looked at his watch. 'I'm just not sure he's going to get us there in time. I know it's a big thing to ask, Dave, but we're country folk, after all, and we know about helping each other. I don't suppose you could take us to the airport? It's out of your way, but—'

'I don't see why not,' said Dad, straightfaced. 'I just need to deal with a small matter first.'

Mr Simpson put his arm around Jubilee. 'You all right to wait awhile, sweetheart?'

Jubilee whipped out a handkerchief and held it to her eyes. 'What if we miss the p-plane? What if Gran d-dies before we get there?'

'I'll be as quick as I can,' said Dad.

He turned back to the driver. 'Are you aware, sir, that it's illegal to carry unsecured livestock?'

The man looked blankly at him.

I know we weren't supposed to say anything. But I couldn't help it. I said, 'A chook. There's a chook on top of your truck.'

Jubilee lowered her hanky. Mr Simpson said, 'This is about a *chicken*? When we're trying to get to my mom's deathbed?' He shook his head as if Dad had disappointed him dreadfully. 'Hennessey, you're not the man I thought you were.'

'Probably not,' said Dad. He shone the torch upwards, so we could all see Clara. Mr Black craned his neck out the window and stared at her.

She waved a wing. Or maybe she was just trying to keep her balance.

'That's against regulations, sir,' said Dad. 'The bird should be in some sort of cage.'

'But – but that's not my chook,' said Mr Black.

Dad's face grew more serious than ever. 'You're carrying *someone else's* chook on top of your truck? Is it a lost chook, sir? Or is it stolen?'

Jubilee buried her face in Mr Simpson's shoulder. 'Oh Gran,' she sobbed.

'Lost,' said Mr Black. 'Definitely lost.'

'In that case,' said Dad, 'I'll have to take it into custody.'

'You do that,' said Mr Black. 'Here, I'll get it down for you.'

He jumped out of the truck, and began to haul himself up the side railings, above the back wheel. When he was high enough, he reached for Clara.

With a loud squawk, she fluttered down to land inside the truck.

Mr Black swore under his breath. Jubilee sobbed louder.

'Seems like you need some help, sir,' said Dad. 'Open up the back of the truck and we'll catch that chook in no time.'

'Look, mate,' said Mr Black, climbing down

again. 'I won't beat about the bush – you've caught me out. It *is* actually my chook.'

'What's her name?' asked Digby.

'Name? Uh – Patsy. Yeah, that's right. Patsy the chook. She's a present for my daughter. It's her birthday, you see. I'm running a bit late because of picking up these passengers, so if you wouldn't mind overlooking this, mate, I'd be very grateful. Don't want to disappoint a little girl, do we?'

'Don't want my mom to die before we get there,' said Mr Simpson in mournful tones. He had a hanky to his eyes now, too.

'Indeed we don't,' said Dad. 'So the truck's empty, apart from the chook?'

'Completely empty,' said the man. 'Not a thing in it. Cleared it out myself, just this afternoon.'

We heard another squawk from inside the truck, followed by a loud bleat.

'That's an odd noise for an empty truck,' said Dad.

'It sounded like a sheep,' Digby said helpfully.

'Well yeah,' said Mr Black, whipping his cap off

and running his fingers through his hair. He didn't sound calm now. 'There's an old ram in there with the chook. Did I forget to mention him? He and the chook are – uh – best friends. Yes, that's it. They never go anywhere without each other. So, because I'm taking the chook, I have to take the ram as well. Sounds daft, I know, but—'

'Are you aware, sir, that you're missing a button from your shirt?' asked Dad.

'What? What's that got to do with—'

'Open the back of the truck, please, sir.'

Mr Black's shoulders sagged, and all the friendliness went out of him. He shuffled around to the back of the truck, undid the bolts and swung the gate open.

Clara was sitting on top of one of the sheep, wobbling back and forth as if she was trying not to fall asleep. When she saw me, she hopped and fluttered and flapped from one sheep to the next, until she was close enough for me to pick her up.

I cuddled her, and she nibbled my collar.

Meanwhile, Dad was shining his torch on one of the sheep's ear tags. 'I believe these sheep were reported stolen a couple of nights ago. How did you come by them, sir?'

Behind us, Mr Simpson cried, 'We were travelling with stolen sheep? I'm sorry, Dave, I was wrong to doubt you. Of course you have to do your duty.' He patted Jubilee's shoulder. 'Sweetheart, we'll just have to hope your gran can hang on until we get there.'

Mr Black fumbled in his pocket and pulled out his wallet. 'Look, mate, I'm sure we can sort this out without too much fuss.' He edged Dad away from me and Digby, and murmured something.

Dad clapped his hand on Mr Black's shoulder and said in a loud voice, 'Derek Black, I am arresting you on suspicion of attempting to bribe a police officer. I am also arresting you on suspicion of theft. You do not have to say anything, but anything you do say may be used in evidence against you.'

Mr Black swore again. Dad reached into the truck and took out the keys. Then he turned to Mr Simpson and said, 'Ernie Simpson, I am arresting you on suspicion of theft. You do not have to say anything, but anything you do say may be used in evidence against you.'

'*What?*' said Mr Simpson. 'Have you gone crazy, Hennessey? Folk told me you were having some problems, but I didn't think you'd lost your mind completely.'

Dad was amazing, Mum, I was so proud of him. He stayed totally calm while Mr Simpson protested and blustered and complained and said he didn't know what the world was coming to when a respectable man and his poor daughter were subjected to this sort of nonsense, and he was going to have Dad fired just as soon as his lawyer got to Little Dismal.

Jubilee wept so loudly that all the sheep woke up and started fussing about being in the back of a truck in the middle of the night. But Dad just held open the back door of the police car really politely, and kept holding it until Mr Black, Mr Simpson and Jubilee climbed in and sat down.

Then he phoned Digby's parents to come and collect the truck, the sheep and Digby.

While we waited for them, I cuddled Clara and whispered, 'You're the best detective in the world, Clara.'

She rested her head on my shoulder and fell asleep.

Love, Olive

Saturday

5.30 AM

I'm too tired for First Squawk, so I do First
Mumble instead. Then I go back to sleep.

7.15 AM

Egg O'Clock. I wake up just in time to lay my
egg in the bottom of Olive's wardrobe. Then I
go back to sleep.

10.00 AM

Olive wakes me up with a plateful of dinner
scraps, and the news that Constable Dad wants
us at the police station.

I eat the scraps, and scurry out to the backyard for a quick Scratch O'Clock. Then I hop up onto the handlebars of Olive's bike, and we ride into town.

10.15 AM

There's a buzz of excitement in Little Dismal. As we ride past the bakery, a man shouts, 'Hey, Olive, I hear your dad caught the stock thief. Good on him!'

'Thieves,' replies Olive. 'There was more than one.'

There's a small crowd of people outside the pub. They cheer as we go past. One of them calls out, 'Hey, Olive, do you know how the Simpsons are? We heard about Ernie's mum getting sick.'

'I reckon they're pretty unhappy right now,' says Olive.

10.20 AM

Constable Dad is leaning back in his chair with his eyes closed. But they snap open when Olive and I enter the police station.

He stares at me. 'Is it true what Olive told me? It really was you who sent the message?'

Olive puts her phone on his desk and I peck out my answer. 'IT'S TRUE.'

Constable Dad chews his lip and looks up at his daughter. 'If this is some sort of joke ...'

'I know it's hard to believe,' says Olive. 'But Clara is really smart. She's a proper detective, Dad.'

One of my feathers is still ruffled from last night's wind. I tuck it into place so I'll look elegant when the television cameras arrive.

Constable Dad shakes his head, then nods. 'Okay, I believe you.' He takes a deep breath and turns to me. 'Clara, I've got Derek Black and Ernie Simpson in the lock-up. I've got the stolen sheep, and the bribery attempt, so Black is going to jail, no question. What I *don't* have is any connection between him and Ernie Simpson, except for Simpson and his daughter being in the truck. Black swears he was working alone and picked the Simpsons up when their car broke down. And Simpson won't say a word apart from reminding me that his lawyer is on his way from Melbourne, and that when he gets here, my career is as good as over.'

'MR SIMPSON TOLD DEREK TO MOVE THE SHEEP LAST NIGHT,' I write.

'That's what I thought,' says Constable Dad. 'But I can't prove it.'

'MR SIMPSON DROVE TO DEREK'S PLACE. I SAW THEM TOGETHER.' I remember an important line from *Amelia X* and add, 'I AM WILLING TO GIVE EVIDENCE IN COURT.'

'Yes, well,' says Constable Dad. 'That could be a problem.'

'WHY?'

'Ah, Olive, could you explain it to her? Please?'

Olive leans towards me and says quietly, 'The court wouldn't listen to a chook. I'm sorry, Clara, but that's the way it is.'

10.45 AM

After all this, Mr Simpson is going to get away with his crimes just because I'm a chook. I can hardly bear the disappointment.

I retreat to the back garden for a sorrowful Dust Bath.

11.00 AM

'Olive Olive Olive! Constable Dad! Olive!' I race back into the police station, squawking their names. I hop up onto the desk. I seize Olive's phone and write, 'WHERE'S THE TRUCK?'

'Locked in the compound,' says Constable Dad.

With another squawk, I dive off the desk and tear out the door.

The locked gate of the compound can't stop a determined detective. I squeeze underneath it, and there's the blue truck, with its back closed.

But that can't stop me either. Not when truth and justice are at stake.

There's a car parked next to the truck, so I fly up onto the bonnet of the car, then onto its roof. From there, it's an easy flight to the back of the truck.

I land on one of the iron bars and peer downwards. Yes, the phone is still there, right where I left it.

I flutter down to the scene of last night's triumph and inspect the phone carefully. It's covered in dust and sheep poo, but otherwise undamaged. I scoop it up in my beak, and prepare to fly up to the iron bars.

But I've barely begun to flap my wings when the back of the truck is pulled open. Constable Dad and Olive are standing there, puzzled.

I dash past them, through the now-open gate and back into the police station. Olive comes running after me. 'What is it?' she asks. 'What have you got?'

I drop the phone on the desk.

'Is that Jubilee's?' Olive thumbs the phone. 'The battery's flat. Hang on.'

She digs in the desk drawer for a charger. Constable Dad walks in, and Olive says, 'Clara's got Jubilee's phone.'

Constable Dad sits on his chair. Olive sits on the desk. I sit on Olive.

We wait patiently for the phone to charge.

11.05 AM

'IS IT CHARGED YET?'

'Not yet.'

11.06 AM

'IS IT CHARGED YET?'

'No, we have to wait a bit longer, Clara.'

11.07 AM

'IS IT CHARGED YET?'

'Just wait, Clara!'

11.15 AM

'IS IT—'

'That should be enough to at least get a look at it,' says Constable Dad.

He lays the phone flat on the desk, and I peck the buttons until I find the right one.

Olive, Constable Dad and I stare at the screen, but all we can see is a man's shoe.

A voice says, 'If I get caught—'

'That sounds like Derek Black,' says Constable Dad.

'You won't get caught,' says a different voice. 'And if you do, I'll get you the best lawyers in the country. As long as you keep your mouth shut.'

'And *that* sounds like Simpson,' murmurs Constable Dad. 'I just wish we could see his face, so he can't wriggle out of it.'

'I'd still rather wait a couple of days,' says Derek, 'until Hennessey's gone.'

'If he's got his eye on me,' says the second voice, 'he might know about you. And it won't be hard to find this place once he starts looking. Get rid of the sheep tonight, and then we all disappear. No more Ernie Simpson. No more Derek Black. No more sheep.' He laughs. 'Not here, anyway.'

A girl's voice cries, 'What are you laughing about? Come and help me look for my phone!'

The shoe moves away from the camera –

and there's Mr Simpson! For just a moment, his face is completely clear. Then he's gone.

Constable Dad slaps the desk. 'We've got him. Well done, Clara! Brilliantly done!'

Olive kisses the top of my head.

I ruffle my feathers modestly and write the words that Inspector Garcia said at the end of Episode 5, 'JUST DOING MY JOB.'

Tuesday night

Dear Mum, Mr Simpson's city lawyer did his best, but he was no match for Dad. And when he saw the video, he stopped talking about suing the police for harassment, and advised Mr Simpson to sit down and say nothing.

And guess what! Dad's been talking to the New South Wales police again, and after a bit of confusion they worked out that the Simpsons are the same people who were pretending to be South African in one town and Irish in another. They had different names each time, and sometimes Jubilee was there (only her name wasn't Jubilee) and sometimes there was a

Mrs Simpson, too (only she wasn't Mrs Simpson).

So they aren't even American.

And it turns out Mr Simpson didn't really buy the pub. He just leased it for a few months, only he never paid the money, and he was about to be thrown out. *And* there's a rumour going around that he was paying off a senior policeman, and that's how he got away with his crimes for so long.

No one in Little Dismal can talk about anything else. They all reckon they suspected him right from the start, because of his 'shifty eyes' and his 'highly unconvincing American accent'. Ha ha. He fooled everyone, and so did Jubilee.

Everyone except Clara.

And you know what? I'm beginning to feel a bit sorry for Jubilee. Her father's in jail waiting for the trial, and that's probably where her mother will end up too, as soon as the police can find her. I don't know what will happen to Jubilee, but she hasn't come back to school.

But I *do* know what will happen to Clara.

I asked Dad if she could live with us permanently, and he said yes, and so did Auntie Gina.

Everyone thinks Dad's a hero, and he is. But Clara's a hero too.

And tomorrow the TV cameras are coming.

Heaps of love
from your Olive

PS. You know who else I'm beginning to feel a bit sorry for? Tracy. She's trying to pretend that she suspected Jubilee all along, and that's why she befriended her, to get to the truth. But no one believes her.

I saw Mrs Savage slip a piece of paper into her hand just before recess today. I bet it was a poem.

Wednesday

5.30 AM

First Squawk. Olive wakes up just in time, and we both squawk so loudly that Constable Dad calls from the kitchen, 'What are you two up to?'

5.45 AM

We practise semaphore together. Olive spells out 'C-L-A-R-A I-S A H-E-R-O'.

8.00 AM

Egg O'Clock. I make my nest on the end of Olive's bed so she won't have to hunt around for her breakfast. There's no school today, not for anyone in Little Dismal. The TV cameras are on their way, and it's a holiday.

Constable Dad has polished his badge and shoes until I can see my reflection in them, and Olive is wearing her best clothes. I have groomed every single feather I could reach. This is my moment. This is everything I have been working towards.

'Olive? Clara?' calls Constable Dad. 'Are you ready?'

9.15 AM

The main street of Little Dismal is lined with people. Digby is there, and so are the Boss and Mrs Savage, the football team, Shorty Davis and his friends, the rest of Olive's class, Mrs Fullerton and Mrs Briggs and dozens of others, all of them cheering as we drive past.

When we reach the police station, the cameras are already there. They start filming as we get out of the car, and a horde of strangers surrounds us, shouting questions.

'Constable Hennessey, tell us how you caught the thieves.'

'Olive, is it true that you helped your father?'

'Constable, how long have you known about the corrupt officer at city headquarters?'

'Olive, what did you think of Jubilee when she first came to school?'

'Constable Hennessey, how did you get the video evidence?'

But one voice rings out above all the others. 'Olive, tell us about your chook. Is it true that she's the real hero of this business?'

A couple of people laugh. Everyone else falls silent. Olive puts her phone on the bonnet of the police car, and I hop out of her arms and land nearby. Constable Dad stands back so the cameras have a clear view of me.

I take three steps towards the phone. One of the camera people whispers, 'This *is* a joke, isn't it?' Someone else whispers, 'Shhh.'

Just a few minutes from now, I will be famous. People all over the country will know who I am. Rufus and Grandmother Polly will let me sit on the top perch, with warm bodies on either side and no one pecking me. I will have friends.

I lower my beak to send a message to the world.

Except – I already have friends. I have Olive and Digby and Constable Dad, who are all much kinder than Rufus and Grandmother Polly. I sleep in Olive's wardrobe and lay my eggs for her breakfast. Tomorrow I'm going to school with her, at the invitation of Mrs Savage, who has hinted to Olive that we are both going to get a special award.

Tomorrow night we are having spaghetti.

If I am famous I will have more friends, but none of them will be as nice as Olive.

If I am famous I will never be able to go undercover again.

A movement on the ground beside the wheel of the police car catches my eye. It's an earwig. No, it's a whole *family* of earwigs!

With a loud squawk, I fly down and start eating them.

When I look up again, Olive is staring at me. I send her a quick semaphore message, 'D-O-N-T G-I-V-E M-E A-W-A-Y.'

She smiles behind her hand and turns back to the cameras. 'Clara is the best chook in the world,' she says. 'But if you want a hero, you need to talk to my dad.'

I snap up the last earwig. Then Olive lifts me in her arms and we set off to find Digby.

THE END

Acknowledgements

Huge thanks to Peter Matheson for his story insights, to my agent Margaret Connolly, who championed Clara from the word go, and to everyone at Allen & Unwin who helped bring her so beautifully to the page, especially Anna McFarlane and Kate Whitfield. Extra special thanks to Cheryl Orsini for the utterly gorgeous illustrations.

About the Author

Lian Tanner has worked as a teacher, a tourist bus driver, a freelance journalist, a juggler, an editor and a professional actor. She has been dynamited while scuba diving and arrested while busking. She once spent a week in the jungles of Papua New Guinea, searching for a Japanese soldier left over from the Second World War. It took her a while to realise that all this was preparation for becoming a writer. Nowadays Lian lives by the sea in southern Tasmania with a handsome tomcat called Harry-le-beau, and a bountiful garden.